Tony gripped the rope until it bit into his palms.

"Willow," he said, hoping he didn't sound like he felt, as if there was a stick of dynamite about ready to explode in his gut.

"Almost there," she said, but he could detect the strain in her voice now. She pulled Carter over the front seat and into the back. He exhaled in relief. All they had to do now was climb out the ruined window. Willow lifted Carter. With his free hand, Tony helped him out. The little boy hopped onto the ground and hugged Tony around the knees.

"Carter..." The word was drowned in the whoosh of earth giving way. The car began to slide over the side.

Tony pushed Carter away and jammed his torso inside the car, where Willow had been thrown off balance. She was scrambling back onto the seat when he reached for her. "Grab my shoulders."

She flung her arms around him.

Dana Mentink is a nationally bestselling author. She has been honored to win two Carol Awards, a HOLT Medallion and an RT Reviewers' Choice Best Book Award. She's authored more than thirty novels to date for Love Inspired Suspense and Harlequin Heartwarming. Dana loves feedback from her readers. Contact her at danamentink.com.

Visit the Author Profile page at LoveInspired.com for more titles.

DEATH VALLEY HIDEOUT

DANA MENTINK

LOVE INSPIRED SUSPENSE

INSPIRATIONAL ROMANCE

LOVE INSPIRED® SUSPENSE

INSPIRATIONAL ROMANCE

ISBN-13: 978-1-335-72307-9

Recycling programs
for this product may
not exist in your area.

Death Valley Hideout

Copyright © 2022 by Dana Mentink

For questions and comments about the quality of this book, please contact us
at CustomerService@Harlequin.com.

Love Inspired
22 Adelaide St. West, 41st Floor
Toronto, Ontario M5H 4E3, Canada
www.LoveInspired.com

Printed in U.S.A.

Bear ye one another's burdens,
and so fulfil the law of Christ.
—*Galatians* 6:2

To Papa Bear, for showing me Death Valley and sharing every adventure with me from here to eternity.

ONE

Willow Duke felt a shiver of uncertainty at her own daring, but she pushed it away as she took the last turn. The wide, smooth drive cut through the flat acres of the airstrip a couple hours east of her own Death Valley hometown. Her anxiety puzzled her. What could be wrong about surprising Tony for his birthday? They'd shifted from acquaintances to friends in the past four months so she figured she knew him well enough to stage a late afternoon birthday treat. Why the worry?

Probably because she'd decided to let someone into her life, and that hadn't happened since the last outsider she'd trusted turned out to be a snake.

But this situation was completely different. She and Tony weren't a couple. Easy friendship, that's what they had. Tony was a widower with two kids to raise; he could use all the friends he could get.

He and Willow were polar opposite temperaments to be sure. Tony was reserved to the point of mysterious, and Willow knew her own ebullient personality could sometimes be too much for the faint of heart. Opposites made for great friends and plenty of fun adventures.

She wiggled her finger in the rearview mirror at Tony's four-year-old son, Carter, strapped into the back in his "big boy seat" as he called it. Facing the opposite direction, his eighteen-month-old sister, Ruby Josephine, nicknamed Bee, kicked off one sock and gurgled. She was a happy baby, regardless of her rough start in life. Willow admired that personality trait. She and Bee were kindred passengers on the optimism train. Just keep chugging, that was Willow's motto.

"Are you holding on to the balloon string real tight, Carter?" she asked, catching his eye in the mirror.

"Uh-huh," he answered, giving the ribbon an experimental tug.

"And you remember what to say when it's time?"

"Happy birthday, Uncle Tony!"

"Uncle Tony?" she said with a laugh. "Don't you mean 'Daddy'?"

Carter's brow puckered and she wondered if she'd hurt his feelings by her laughter. Where had he come up with uncle? Tony didn't have any siblings. Strange. Muscles deep in her stomach tensed.

Carter's brow was crimped as he stared at the airstrip coming into view. "We'll shout happy birthday, and he'll be so surprised," she said. Again a tendril of tension tightened inside her. Sure Tony hadn't meant for her to overhear his phone call that afternoon revealing that he was heading to the airstrip, nor probably expected she'd made note of his birthday from the driver's license he'd dropped in the store. He spent a good amount of time at the airstrip, where he'd gotten a job flying tourist helicopters after his navy retirement, so it was the perfect place to plan a birthday surprise. Yet his tone on the phone when he'd been setting up the meeting hadn't exactly been friendly nor businesslike, she recalled as she scrolled through her memory. There was something in it she could not quite identify, something almost like anger, though the words themselves had been civil.

Was it a mistake to join him if he would be having a difficult meeting? But who wouldn't love a surprise birthday greeting from their two adorable children? And Willow and the kids had been bored anyway, once the Play-Doh was done and the chunky crayon coloring was completed. Too hot to play outside that afternoon until the 110-degree temps cooled. The Mojave Desert was no gentle climate in June. Maybe if she was more practiced at watching the kids, she'd know how else to entertain them. She didn't care for them often. Tony had a reliable neighborhood lady for that. But he'd needed a favor, and she'd agreed without a second thought.

Tony will love his birthday treat, she reassured herself. His serious face would break into that smile, the unguarded one she'd only witnessed sporadically in the four months she'd known him. He was always so busy…too scheduled even to meet her twin brother, Levi, in Furnace Falls. Levi had extended an invitation after Willow explained how Carter would love riding horses on her brother's ranch. Well what single dad wouldn't be busy with a career to manage and two small kiddos to tend to? There was something sweet and quiet about Tony that made her want to help him, or maybe it was the adorable children who accompanied them almost everywhere.

His wife had died in a car accident when Bee was a newborn, so it made sense he would want to have them around whenever possible. Aside from their "nanny," a sweet older lady in town, he'd only left them with Willow. She was honored, and maybe flattered too. Carter liked her, and the feeling was mutual. Bee loved everyone, and it was a pleasure to hold and rock the little girl with the cutest button nose in the universe.

The sun was low in the sky, trapped behind the distant foothills, sending long shadows across the road as she drove. She rolled down the Jeep's window to test for a breeze. No visitors to speak of, she thought, as she pulled into a parking space near the welcome center. The paint was dingy and the cement porch cracked, but the sign was cheerful… Welcome to Desert Air Excursions. Tony's helicopter was a sleek black Bell Ranger with a red tail and rear rotor. Her brother Austin, a plane afficionado and pilot himself, asked to see it every single time she brought up Tony in conversation. At least Austin was too preoccupied with his new wife and their four dogs to badger her about it lately.

Tony was probably just shy, she thought, like Levi, her quiet twin.

The sinking sun blazed so brightly through her windshield that she had to shade her eyes. It took a moment before she realized that Tony was striding out of the visitor center through a side entrance, hands on hips. She was ready to put her plan into motion when she noticed there was another man following him, with a similar lanky build and sandy hair. They charged out into the heat, one after the other until Tony stopped and spun toward his companion. The conversation did not appear to be a friendly one. She put a hand on the ignition to activate the window button so they wouldn't be eavesdropping, but the sentence stopped her.

"You can't go on the run with them," Tony yelled. "Man up, for once in your life."

On the run? Tony's voice was steeped in rage, so unlike anything she'd ever heard from him before. The other man turned on Tony, shoulders pitched forward as if he was expressing himself heatedly, but she could not hear what he said. Walk away from what?

The two men were closer together now, feet apart from each other, and she could not help but notice how similar they looked. Almost as if they were...brothers. The tingle of unease increased into a flash of foreboding. If they were brothers, then Tony had been lying to her about being an only child. And what else? His dead wife? Carter had called him Uncle Tony.

Suddenly it seemed her plan to surprise him was a very, very bad idea.

Carter wiggled in the backseat. She had more immediate problems. What was she going to do? Starting the car would draw attention, but she couldn't exactly about-face and leave with Carter hanging on to his daddy's birthday balloon. As much as she wanted to slink away to think, that was out of the question with the two kids accompanying her.

Wait, she thought. They'll go back inside in a minute and she could figure out how to proceed then, but Carter was already undoing his car seat straps.

"We have to stay in the car until Daddy is finished."

Carter did not appear to hear. Now he was peering out the window. "It's Daddy," he said, small hand pressed to the glass. "Bee, it's Daddy."

"Just one minute, Carter. We have to wait until the grown-ups are done talking, okay?"

But then she heard the door unlatch. "Stay put, Carter," she said more sternly, but he was already out of the car. She thrust open her own door and hopped out in an effort to catch him. "Stop," she said. Too late. The child slid out on the tarmac.

"Daddy," he called, running now, the balloon trailing behind him.

Both men jerked to look at the boy. She couldn't hear what they said, but Tony half raised his arms as if he would try and stop him. Her grand idea had gone from bad to worse. She started to follow Carter, still trying to draw him back.

Carter had crossed half the distance, when an engine roared, loud in the thin air, as another car raced onto the tarmac. She couldn't see the driver through the blistering sun. A guest reporting for a tour? Surely not at this hour, at that speed. When the vehicle pulled closer, she saw the driver's side window of the sedan opening.

A nightmare unrolled before her eyes as a gun was aimed out the window. Dreaming, she had to be dreaming. It could not be a gun, not really.

Like a slow-motion clip from a movie, she saw an arm extend, wrist bare and hairy, gun nestled in the fingers. And then there was a flash and bang. Carter stumbled. Terror seized her heart in a vise-like grip. Had he been shot, or had he tripped? Horror froze her in place for a second, and then she was running, screaming Carter's name, entreating God with everything in her that the child had not been hurt.

The man Tony had been talking to ducked under the belly of the helicopter as the intruder's car screeched to a stop. Now Tony was running too, his long legs eating up the distance as he raced toward Carter.

But the shooter fired again. Tony hit the

ground a fraction of a second before, the bullet flying over his head. Willow screamed as she dropped to her knees, rolling into a ball, listening to several more shots punching holes into the asphalt to her right. The car rolled by. Possibly after the man who'd run away? Crawling, the hot asphalt burning her palms, she continued on toward Carter, who was sitting up, tears streaming down his cheeks.

"Carter, I'm coming," she screamed again. Rocks bit into her palms and the knees of her jeans. She was almost there when the car with the shooter backed up. Her breath froze as he reversed, coming to a stop between her and the boy. Another shot in her direction made her curl up and cover her head again. She heard Carter squeal. By the time she got her legs to lift her from the ground, the car was retreating into the setting sun.

It took a moment for her to comprehend. Carter was gone. The gunman had swept him up and taken him. A security guard barreled up in a marked car, but she barely saw him.

Tony ran to her, brown eyes electric with fear, judgment in his words as he gripped her shoulders. "Why did you bring them here, Willow?" he asked through gritted teeth.

Why? She could not rally an answer just

then. Her mind was somewhere else, with the terrified boy she'd brought into chaos.

"Get back to the car," he snapped. "Take Bee somewhere safe." Then he was sprinting to the helicopter. She heard the sound of flipping switches, and less than three minutes later the whine of the rotors as he coaxed the aircraft to life. Covering her ears, she crouched with the security guard as the *thwop, thwop* of the blades shook the ground.

In a moment, the helicopter roared out of sight, wheeling in the direction of the kidnapper's car. The shock settled slowly around her as her senses struggled to take in what had happened.

Carter's balloon drifted away into the sky. The security guard was radioing the police. In a fog she stumbled back to the car. Bee was crying, wailing until her cheeks were red, scared from the noise and the screaming. Willow lifted her from the back and retrieved her beloved stuffed toy, a cow named Moo Moo. "It's okay, Bee. Don't you worry." She wanted to say nice things like 'your brother will be fine' and 'Daddy will bring him back,' but she could not push the words over the impenetrable wall of fear. Bee eventually subsided to a whimper, stuck her two fingers in her mouth and began to suck them.

The guard approached. "Cops will be here soon. Is the baby hurt? Are you?"

Hurt? How could she describe what she was feeling, the anguish.

Why did you bring them here?

An innocent reason, but she'd brought them nonetheless, when he'd expected her to watch them at his safe little home.

She was the reason Carter had been snatched by the gunman. What if Tony lost them? If the car turned down a road he could not see from the air? What would happen then to the young boy who was her responsibility?

"Let's get you both inside the building to wait for the cops." The guard held out a hand to her.

Without any more thought, she thrust Bee into the startled arms of the security guard. "Keep her safe. I have to go."

"Wait a minute…" he called after her but she did not stop. Leaping back into the car, she cranked on the engine and floored the gas.

Tony hadn't completed any of the normal preflight warm-up routine. There wasn't a second to spare. As soon as the N1 gauge hit 58 percent, he'd released the button on the throttle and urged the bird into the air. In five additional minutes, he'd locked onto the kidnapper's location, tracking the progress of the car as it sped through the canyon. His pulse pounded so hard it almost drowned out the noise of the rotors. He should have realized the moment his brother showed up there would be others right behind, ready to kill. But the children weren't supposed to be anywhere close. It shouldn't have happened.

A million insults poured through his head at his brother's dumb choices, but he tried to shove them aside. The fallout of what Ron had done would be catastrophic for Bee and Carter, for himself, maybe even for Willow, but he didn't dare consider that. Willow's choice, albeit unwittingly, had put them directly in the crosshairs.

Why had she brought the kids? If only she'd listened to him when he'd asked her to keep them in. Her impulsive nature, so unlike his own, was why she'd stood out to him in the first place. He wanted to blame her, but the truth burned at him.

You messed up, Tony. You never should have let her into your life. You can't afford to have friends. Period.

He looked below and spotted the black car speeding into a rocky canyon. The overhanging boulders and the failing sunlight obscured his view, offering only glimpses as the vehicle appeared every few moments. Was Carter in the front seat? The back? Hurt? Or worse?

Tony was trained to stay cool in difficult situations from his years as a Forest Service pilot, so he did his best to shove down his rising panic. If the guy had wanted to kill Carter, he wouldn't have bothered snatching him.

Unless he changes his plan.

Tony swallowed, throat sand dry, and gripped the control.

Carter's best chance, his only chance, hinged on Tony keeping the car in sight. When the driver stopped, Tony would be there. Another flicker of headlights appeared on the road a mile or so behind the kidnapper's car. He did a double take. Willow? Unbelievable.

"Turn around before you or Bee gets hurt," he hollered to no one. She should be back at the airstrip with the police, he thought savagely.

The two cars continued on, whisking around the turns in and out of the rocky canyon walls. Fortunately, the Bell was fully fueled to take the next day's passengers on a flying tour around the outskirts of the Death Valley National Park and surrounds.

The danger of his own behavior preyed on him. Flying this fast would not be safe as they exited the canyon territory and headed into the more populated areas. He wouldn't be able to pursue and though the local police would no doubt be dispatched they did not understand the situation they were dealing with. He'd have to break off his pursuit and then what would happen to Carter? Would he be a bargaining chip? Or an example of what would happen to them all in time?

He battled down a more violent surge of panic. There would be no bargaining. The person that Ron had crossed was not interested in making deals, only in revenge. Killing them was the way to punish his brother. His cramped fingers forced him to try and relax his grip on the controller.

The situation was critical and there was only one thing to do. Stop the driver before Tony lost Carter forever. *Think, Tony. Figure it out.*

Two miles north, he knew from his many flights over the desert, the road dropped down into a narrow basin between two upthrust rock walls. It was a small space, too small for a normal safe landing of a chopper, but this wasn't normal and his own safety was no longer the weightiest factor in the equation. Carter was all that mattered and stopping Willow's risky pursuit before she or Bee got hurt. Willow's face on that tarmac, a mask of terror and confusion…would be forever carved into his memory. *She's in this because of your lies. Some friend, Tony.*

Mentally he calculated the impact of the wind that would funnel through the mountain pass and cause turbulence for the helo. Landing the craft in unknown conditions was a reminder of his previous life, when he'd flown into burning forests that no normal pilot would ever attempt. His previous life, when he'd chosen who he'd wanted to be…

You were a good pilot, then. And you'd better be good now. Anger tightened his muscles and he forced himself to relax as he pitched away from the road.

Why was he required to pay for the poor decisions of someone else? Why was Carter? That picture of Willow resurfaced again. Hadn't he taken away some of her choices with his lies? His own hypocrisy left a bitter taste in his mouth. "Lord, Almighty," he prayed. "I'm gonna need some help here." He felt the stony determination replace the fear.

I can save both of them, he thought stubbornly.

I can, and I will.

Jaw tight and teeth gritted, he started to take the helicopter down.

TWO

The lights from Tony's helicopter crawled over Willow's car as she pushed the speed as fast as she dared. They had ascended to a twisting road carved through a canyon. Ahead the sedan was taking the turns at such a fast clip that the rocks spun out from under the tires and sailed off the road and down the cliff side. If the driver lost control...

She squeezed the steering wheel to will away the thought. Her plan was simple to the point of childish. *Catch up and don't let him go.* It wasn't much, but Willow had always done her best work under pressure. Something would occur to her, it had to. Carter's life was on the line because of her, and there was no second-guessing her decision to follow.

Snippets of gunfire, Carter's cries, the squeal of tires ricocheted in her head. She had literally delivered the children right in the middle of a shooting gallery.

How could she have known? The thing that shook her most was Tony's expression. He had been expecting trouble, maybe not in the form of a shooter, but trouble, nonetheless. But Tony was a retired navy pilot, a quiet man raising his two children, content with a simple small-town life. Wasn't he? And was the man with Tony a relation?

Bee, it's Daddy. Could Carter have been talking about the second man?

Maybe the resemblance was a trick of the light. There were very few photos hanging in Tony's small apartment, a fact she'd teased him about since she was a photographer and there was never enough wall space to display all the family photos she'd taken over the years.

Why did you bring them here? A chill invaded her limbs and sank deep into her bones.

The car ahead shimmied around the corner, the rear tires skidding dangerously on the narrow road, sending rivulets of loose debris spraying over the side. She dropped back a few feet. A crash here would send them over the cliff side and who knew what injuries Carter's little body might sustain? She doubted he was even buckled into the seat belt.

Was he holding on tight? Was he crying?

Ahead the lights of Tony's helicopter disappeared into the distance. The darkness closed in around her. There was no way he was calling off the pursuit. What was he planning? Maybe the police had constructed some sort of roadblock, but would they have had the time? She had no choice but to keep her foot on the accelerator.

They raced around a turn and then up toward a sharp crag. Her Jeep engine whined at the steep grade. At the top, it appeared to level out, but she knew from experience it would then drop down into a shallow depression, an area of no more than a hundred feet wide, before it climbed back up and lost itself in the cliffs again.

No, she thought. *Tony can't be planning to land there.* During the unofficial flying lessons her brother had administered, she'd learned that landing without having surveyed the area was hazardous in the extreme, and the canyon walls would funnel the air back at the helicopter in unexpected ways if a pilot tried to land in such a place. The space was too small, too inhospitable to attempt to put the helicopter down, especially when there were just a few wan streaks of daylight left, painting the landscape in shifting shadow.

The car she was following braked hard when they hit the plateau and she did too.

A second later she understood why. A roar

of turbulent wind blew rocks and grit in all directions. She blinked incredulously as she watched Tony fight the air currents to land the helicopter. One tiny slip and the rotor would clip a rock and crash, or the skids could sink into the sandy debris and pitch the aircraft onto its nose.

Frozen in shock, she watched through the whirling bits of debris that peppered her windshield. Once, she cried out as he seemed to land on one skid and then he rose again like someone testing the depth of an unknown body of water. The second time he brought the helicopter to rest and she heard the sound of the rotors powering down. Relief swamped her senses. He'd actually done it. The feeling didn't last long.

He leaped from the helicopter, running at full speed as he charged up the slope toward the waiting car, which was hemmed in by Willow's. She felt like screaming at him to take cover. He would be an easy target when he emerged at the top of the slope.

The driver stepped out of the car. Willow gulped. His gun was pointed at Tony's head.

Ducking low below the dashboard she hit the horn.

The gunman flinched only for a moment, then shifted and fired in her direction. The bullet punched through her front window and the next scream froze in her throat.

When she dared to risk a look, he'd swiveled his attention back to the road where Tony erupted into sight again, head bent low and running fast. The gunman fired off two more shots. Tony dove to the shoulder and rolled behind some rocks. The shots continued in a wild arc alternating between Tony's direction and hers. A shot disintegrated Willow's side mirror. She ducked under the dash. The shooter continued peppering the ground until she heard the click through the broken window glass. She eased up cautiously.

The gunman swore and jammed a hand in his pocket. He would have to reload. Tony must have realized it too, because he was on his feet and running again straight toward the abductor's car. With a sick feeling, Willow realized he wasn't going to make it in time. There was too much ground to cover and the gunman was already sliding a fresh clip into the chamber.

Willow's position was closer, but there was no way she could overpower the man. He was broad across the chest and stocky, black hair curling around his big head.

All right, plan B, she thought. While the man was focused on his gun, she crept from the car, keeping behind the open door as best she could. Heart hammering against her ribs, she scooped up a handful of dirt. With a sudden movement, she lunged forward and flung it in his eyes. He reeled back, pawing the grit away. Before he could recover, she followed up with another fistful of dirt and a coffee cup from her car, whatever she could find to hurl at him. He'd staggered back a step to regroup.

Seeing his opportunity, Tony knocked him down with a flying tackle. The gun came loose and spun through the air. She tried to see where it had gone, but she couldn't make it out in the gloom. Tony and the shooter were locked together, rolling over repeatedly, grunting with the effort. Willow could not tell which man was getting the upper hand. What should she do? Find the gun? She wanted to creep forward to get Carter out of the other vehicle, but she wasn't sure how to get around the two wrestling men.

The gunman made it to his feet in a boxer's stance, and Tony sprang up a second later, fists up as well.

The man dealt Tony a vicious blow to the side of his head, which sent him staggering backward. Then the gunman spun around, probably looking for his gun without finding it, whirling in time to throw up an arm to block

Tony's incoming punch. They moved nearer to the cliff's edge.

"Watch out," she called to Tony, but she wasn't sure he heard her. Tony went in again, this time with a strike to the stomach. The blow sent the gunman staggering back. The ground under his feet slipped away as he neared the cliff edge; arms wheeling, he fell into the yawning darkness and disappeared.

She blinked to be sure she wasn't imagining it, but the threat was gone, just that quickly.

Tony, panting hard, bent at the waist to catch his breath.

Her lungs fought for oxygen too. She wanted to cheer, to throw up her hands in victory, but all she could think about was Carter.

After another few seconds, Tony too was moving toward the abductor's car, a trickle of blood from his nose gleaming. Willow was ahead of him, a sense of dread spreading down her spine. Something was wrong, her instincts shouted. She could not at first pinpoint what it was. With a sickening realization, it dawned on her. The abductor's car had been parked parallel to the road, perilously close to the edge. As she got closer, she saw to her horror that the vehicle was slowly sliding toward the drop-off as the ground gave way underneath it with a low screech.

This can't be happening, she thought.

But it was. Even as she ran, the car was slipping toward the same deadly plunge the gunman had taken.

Tony swiped the blood from his nose and blinked away the dizziness as he tried to catch up to Willow. His mind was on the gunman. Had he fallen to his death? Was he curled up on the slope, ready to regroup? He almost plowed right into her when she stopped abruptly. Irritated, he wanted to scoot her out of the way. Everything in him was screaming to tear open the car door and reassure himself that Carter was okay.

But Willow had grabbed his arm, her fingers digging into his biceps. "It's sliding," she said.

Sliding? What was she talking about? At first, he thought he'd misheard, until he detected the soft sound of the rocks sloughing away from under the wheels. He froze. Now he got it. The car was teetering over the cliff edge, the driver's side already suspended out in the air.

He was momentarily stunned and then he snapped into action, hurrying to yank at the front passenger door. Locked. He tried the rear passenger door with the same result. If he attempted to creep around and get in the driver's side, his weight would take it right over. The car was swaying like a teeter-totter now, as more and more earth gave way beneath it.

A gleam of white moved inside the car. Carter's face appeared from the front seat near the steering wheel. Tony's fear about the car plunging over the cliff almost eclipsed his joy that the boy was alive. He needed to figure out how to keep him that way. Carter's fingers were pressed to his mouth, so tiny, his eyes dark pools in the gloom.

"Hold on, Carter. I'm going to get you out of there," Tony shouted. Then he tried to gentle his tone. "Can you open the door, buddy?"

Carter looked down and Tony could hear him straining. "I'm stuck," he wailed.

Willow looked through the passenger window that was partially open. "His foot is caught between the seats."

The child began to yank harder, his whimpers audible. How could he get Carter out before the whole thing slid over the cliff? "It's okay, Carter. Can you reach out your arms so we can pull you out?"

The child complied, leaning far enough that Tony could grab his hand, but pulling didn't release him. Carter started to cry.

"Hey, don't worry, buddy. It's okay. If you can't come out, we'll come in and get you."

Willow had run to her car, returning with a ball-peen hammer, which she handed to Tony. "We're gonna break the glass to get you out. Move back and cover your face, okay?" she called to Carter. He scrunched down and held his arms over his eyes.

It took three attempts before the gizmo did the job, and the remaining glass shattered into hundreds of tiny cubes. Tony reached in to find the door release. "I can't override it from here," he said, his mounting fear like a rock in his belly. "It has to be done from the driver's side." There was no choice. "I'll climb in..."

He reached for the edge of the window and got himself in up to the shoulders, when he felt the car start to give under his weight. Quickly he withdrew, heart pounding. It teetered, sliding a few more inches toward the drop.

"I'll do it," Willow said, startling him. She wasn't waiting for him to approve the plan. She was already taking off her jacket.

"No," he tried to say.

She ignored him. "I'm lighter than you are. There's a rope in the back of my car. You can tie it to the tow hitch of my Jeep and steady us that way."

"Willow," he tried again, but she whirled on him, eyes flashing in the night.

"Do you have a better plan, Tony?" The

words hung in the air, a slight defiance around the word *Tony*.

"No," he said, biting back whatever he'd been about to say. "I don't."

"All right then, hurry. This thing's not going to hold much longer."

The word *hurry* snapped him out of his stupor, or maybe it was the urgency in her tone. He sprinted to get the rope and fastened it to the Jeep before he helped her tie the other end around her waist. He wasn't fooling himself. It was a feeble effort at best. If the car slipped and Willow and Carter were caught on something inside, both of them would go sliding into the canyon, like the gunman had, regardless of their makeshift safety rig. Sweat slicked his hands, and he wiped them on his jeans.

Before he could say another word, she was at the busted rear passenger window.

"Carter," she was calling in an impossibly soothing voice. "I'm going to come in right now, sweetie. We'll get your foot unstuck, and we'll climb out together."

Tony saw Carter nod, but as he did so the car lurched and the boy was thrown against the seat. His whimper carried to Tony, who clutched the rope, every nerve and sinew wire taut as he prayed with all his might. Willow waited until the car stopped moving.

"Oopsy," Willow said. "That didn't work, huh? All right. I'm going to reach over the front seat and help you, okay?"

As the car steadied, Willow crawled the rest of the way in. He could hear her chatting with Carter in a calm, light voice. Her self-control was a breathtaking contrast to his. His body craved to dive in and pull them free. Instead he clung to the rope. Slowly, painfully slowly, she reached over the front seat.

"Ah. Well you really did get that foot stuck, didn't you? Tell you what. I'm going to untie your lace and we'll just pull your foot right out of that silly shoe. You said they were shoes for babies anyway, right? We can get something with race cars on them. Or maybe some cowboy boots like my brother has."

There was no answer from Carter.

Willow moved slowly, with the grace of a ballet dancer as she leaned over the front seat. Tony heard the ominous cascade of soil giving way under the car. He gripped the rope until it bit into his palms, more out of fear than usefulness. "Willow," he said, hoping he didn't sound like he felt, as if there was a stick of dynamite about ready to explode in his gut.

"Almost there," she sang out, but he could detect the strain in her voice now. She pulled Carter over the front seat and into the back. He exhaled in relief. All they had to do now was climb out the ruined window. Willow lifted Carter. With his free hand, Tony helped him out. The little boy hopped onto the ground and hugged Tony around the knees.

"Carter..." The word was drowned in the whoosh of earth giving way. The car began to slide over the side.

Tony pushed Carter to the side and jammed his torso inside the car where Willow had been thrown off balance. She was scrambling back onto the seat when he reached for her. "Grab my shoulders."

She flung her arms around him and he shoved against the pull of gravity, straining toward the broken window. Metal screamed all around him. He hauled them both past the broken glass and out onto the ground.

With the earth trembling underneath them, they scrambled up. Willow threw off the rope, Tony grabbed Carter under the arms and the three of them ran away from the dissolving earth. The car tumbled and crashed down the cliff side until it came to rest, a crumpled mass at the bottom. Safe, they huddled together, panting hard.

"Are you hurt, buddy?" Tony asked.

The boy shook his head, shivering.

Tony turned to Willow. "Are you okay?"

"Yes." She shook bits of glass from her clothes and shoved back her tangled hair.

"Is Bee in your car?" he said.

"She's at the airstrip with the security guard," Willow said, panting. "What do we do now? Wait for the police?"

Wait out in the open? Sitting like ducks on a pond while the goons had a chance to regroup? "No, we have to go to town, get you and Carter to a doctor for a check. I'll fly the chopper back later. We'll take your car since we've got Carter's baby seat."

"Big boy seat," Carter and Willow corrected at exactly the same moment.

Impossibly, Tony smiled. "Right. Big boy seat."

Willow climbed into the back so she could hold Carter's hand. He was sniffling, not talking much, but she kept up a steady one-sided conversation, meant to distract him from thinking about what he'd endured, he figured. The crash of the car slamming into the rocks echoed through his memory. A couple of seconds later would have been too late.

"Maybe we can find some ice cream at the hospital," Willow was saying to Carter.

Thoughts of ice cream would distract Carter.

If only Tony could push what had happened out of his mind, but the truth was the threat wasn't over, not by a mile.

THREE

Willow's medical check at the local clinic was thorough but quick. Her minor scrapes were bandaged and the cut on her hand cleaned and wrapped, not deep enough to require stitches. Tony waved off an exam, accompanied Carter into the doctor's cubicle while she sat in her torn jeans, face dirty and hair tangled, waiting for some sort of explanation about what had just happened.

Tony hadn't wanted to talk in the car in front of Carter, so her million questions burned, unanswered.

Who had come after Tony and kidnapped Carter? Who was the man Tony'd been meeting with? Police officers trickled in, a few at a time. They took her information and some details about what had happened, but she got the oddest sense they were holding back, glancing at each other as if they were unsure how to proceed. Her sheriff cousin, Jude, would have said, "Waiting for the bigger brass." Who would that be? Why did she feel like everyone was hiding something from her?

When Tony emerged, he and Carter were bundled directly into a police car and she into a second one. The cop behind the wheel was cordial but refused to tell her anything except, "You're wanted at the station to give a full statement."

"Where is Bee? I mean, the baby, Ruby Josephine?"

"I can't say, ma'am."

"Why can't you? Has she been taken home? Who's watching her?"

"Like I said…"

"I know, I know," she finished with a huff. "You can't say."

She was escorted into the local police station and left to sit in a chair in a conference room by herself. The room must have been a bunker in a former life, since she could not get any kind of signal on her cell phone. Pacing helped until she began to feel the ache of muscles pulled in the rescue and resumed her chair. Finally, when her patience departed and she was about to leave and drive herself to find Bee, statement or no, the door opened. Tony came in, a bandage on his neck, dust coating his hair, followed by two uniformed officers.

As soon as she saw the US Marshals badge on the chest of the dark-eyed woman, she knew her life was about to be upended. Marshals wouldn't be involved unless there was a very good reason. It took all her effort to keep from staring at Tony, trying to ferret out the truth on his face.

"US Marshal Diaz," the woman said. "And this is Sheriff Rocklin Severe."

A heavyset mustached man in a local police uniform bobbed his chin at her. "Hello, ma'am."

"I've heard your name," Willow said. "You took over in Furnace Falls for my cousin Jude."

"Only temporarily," he said, a smile twitching his mustache. "When he's done with his training, I'll ride off into the sunset. Jude's got no intention of giving up his saddle."

"Why are you here handling this case with the marshals?" she asked.

He offered another lazy smile. "We'll get to that in a minute."

Willow shot a glance at Tony. His mouth was pinched, arms folded tight across his muscled chest. He did not meet her gaze.

"Is Carter okay?"

Now he did look at her, his expression unreadable. "Yes," he said. "Thank you for getting him out of that car. He's scared and scratched up, but not injured." She waited for him to add something, but he didn't.

Willow sat up straight. "All right. Shall we get to the meat and potatoes, as my cousin Beckett would say? Who is going to tell me what is going on here?"

Diaz leaned against the table, her arms also folded. She was likely in her early forties. Her short dark hair was bobbed, and she was fit and all business. "You were embroiled in a situation that you never should have been exposed to." Diaz flicked the quickest of glances at Tony. "Since this whole thing is sputtering like a backfiring engine, we're going to have to come clean with her."

"And then what?" Tony snapped. "I slink off somewhere and start all over again?"

Diaz arched a brow. "Don't shoot the messenger. I don't deserve it."

"I don't either, and neither does Willow." Tony sighed from somewhere deep in his body.

He looked bone-deep weary. It almost made her feel sorry for him.

"Which is exactly why," Diaz said, "you shouldn't have allowed her to become involved."

"Excuse me," Willow said. "Can we please stop talking like I'm not in the room? What is going on? Someone spell it out for me, and we can save a bunch of time."

"All right," Diaz said. "The man you know sitting here next to you as Tony Ortega is actually Anthony Martin."

Martin? She stared at Tony. All the tiny inconsistencies she'd noted over the past four months weren't coincidental after all. Her instincts had whispered that he was a liar, but she hadn't listened. *Wow, Willow. Way to go.*

Diaz continued. "His brother, Ron Martin, was an accountant for an extremely dangerous man named Otto Gaudy, who created a dark web store. It's a clearinghouse on the internet for all things illicit and dangerous. Everything can be bought or sold, regardless of legalities. Drugs, guns, etc., and there are people out there who will do anything you want, also regardless of legalities, like hit men and crooked doctors. You name it. The dark web is a cesspool for the dregs of humanity, and Gaudy profits hand over fist from it."

The dark web? What had she stepped into when she became Tony's friend? Was Tony involved in such things too?

Diaz continued. "Gaudy went to trial, and Ron was willing to testify against him. The judge had a family emergency and issued a two-week postponement. Ron used the break to take off. He left a note saying he had no faith in law enforcement and he was going to take matters into his own hands."

"I tried to talk him out of it when he contacted me," Tony said.

"Too bad," Diaz said. "The US Marshals provided protection for Ron during the trial and entered his brother, Tony, here, who was caring for Ron's children, into WITSEC."

Uncle Tony.

"It was supposed to be temporary, until Gaudy was convicted," Tony said. "And then he would take them back, but my brother neglected to tell anyone that he'd also stolen documents from Gaudy for blackmail purposes as a backup plan. That's what he means by 'taking things into his own hands.' What's more, he…" Tony's cheeks flushed. "He had a relationship with Gaudy's wife, Eugenia."

Willow realized she'd gasped aloud. "What a mess."

"Our sentiments exactly," Diaz resumed. "The trial is set to recommence two weeks from this Friday, but we're not going to get a conviction with a no-show witness. Short story is we need Ron for his testimony. And if the blackmail papers are real, they might help us get a slam dunk. But it could be Ron's lying in an effort to save his skin." She shot a look at Tony. "Ron's a champion liar."

"If he was lying, why would Gaudy send a hit man to kill Tony or take Carter?" Willow asked.

Diaz looked at Willow as if she was a kid on her first day of class. "Stopping Ron from testifying and or handing over evidence is only half of it. Gaudy is going to make an example of Ron so no one will ever cross him again. Make no mistake. It will be a violent, bloody example. From your description, we believe the hit man is Devon Klee. He's experienced. Let's leave it at that."

Willow was only half taking it in. She could not help but stare at the man she'd thought was Tony Ortega. He wasn't who he said he was, wasn't even the father of the two children, so the dead wife must be a fabrication too. Lies. Their whole friendship had been nothing but lies. Clearly, she'd gotten no wiser at spotting a liar since her last go-around. Her shame set a match to her anger.

"So you used me," she said to him, interrupting Diaz. "Why? You needed someone to watch your kids? Run out of babysitters?" She could not keep the bitterness from her voice.

"No," he said to his lap. "That wasn't it."

"Got lonely with your fake identity so you

needed company?" Still he didn't look at her, but she wondered if she was getting closer to the truth. Great. So she'd merely been a convenient chum. It explained why he'd never wanted to visit Furnace Falls or take the kids to the ranch. She knew her cheeks were flaming.

She got up with as much dignity as she could muster. "All right. Thanks for the information." She turned to Tony. "The kids are amazing, and they deserve a stable life. I hope it works out for you." And then she marched to the door.

"There's a way to save the children," Diaz called after her. "A chance Tony can get his life back."

Willow stopped short of the threshold. "How? Ron's run away."

Diaz pursed her lips. "First you have to know that Gaudy will never let up. He's not the kind of man to forget being crossed. The last person who blabbed about the details of a dark web transaction was found at the bottom of a well courtesy of Devon Klee."

Her stomach churned. "And you think he'll come after Tony and the kids even though they had nothing to do with Ron's actions?" Willow demanded. It was not in her nature to accept that any situation was hopeless.

"You want my take on it?" Diaz said. "The

only way Ron is going to get Gaudy off his back is to put him away for good. If he runs, Gaudy will find him eventually, no matter where, no matter when. If he attempts blackmail, it will just speed up his execution. His only choice is to come back and testify at the trial." She paused. "You can help, Willow."

"Me? How?" Willow eyed Diaz and then the door. Should she keep listening? Allow herself to be drawn further into the mess? Carter's terrified face kept poking at her, the balloon he'd so carefully selected drifting away into the darkness. Would he and Bee really always be at risk? What was the right choice?

Diaz watched her closely. "I have an idea how to keep Tony and the kids safe until Ron comes back."

"This doesn't concern her anymore," Tony said. "I can take care of things myself."

"No, you can't. You need a quiet place to hole up and the help of a local." Diaz added, "And besides, Klee might have seen Willow clearly enough to identify her. If he did…" She let the sentence trail off.

If he did, she was a target. But maybe he hadn't. The lighting wasn't good, and she'd been throwing everything she could find at him. Even if he had, she had her own personal army of brothers and cousins for protection. She could walk away and her involvement would be over. She looked again at the door. Help Tony?

Tony did not watch her. He was staring at his clasped hands, jaw tight.

Diaz shook her head. "Tony can't run away from this, not with two little kids. He needs help, Willow. Your help."

She heaved out a breath. "I'm going to splash some water on my face. If I decide to come back, I'll return in a few minutes. If I don't, then you can consider that a 'no' from me."

Ron's plan to blackmail Gaudy had disaster written all over it. He had to testify, but she did not see what any of it had to do with her. *You were a temporary babysitter. Wrong time, wrong place.* But she'd been a witness to Carter's abduction and Klee would have murdered Tony without her interference. Stay or go? As she found the tiny restroom, she feared it would take a lot more than a dash of cold water for her to figure out what to do.

Diaz was taunting him, dangling the carrot. Get his life back? His deepest desire. He stood up and started pacing the confines of the drab room. Tantalizing as it was to consider whatever plan Diaz was cooking up, he didn't like the idea of roping Willow in to help. He'd done enough damage already to her life. She would have been shot, in a car wreck, tumbled over the cliff side, except for God's intervention. Lesson learned, not to be repeated. A headache was building behind his temple, and he would have slammed down some aspirin if given the chance. She would be right to leave him, them, drive away without looking back. He more or less hoped she did.

But after five minutes the door opened and she walked back in, strawberry blond hair neatened, freckled cheeks free of the dirt from their near catastrophe. He all but gaped. Maybe she'd returned to tell him off like he deserved.

Calmly, she resumed her seat. "I thought it over and prayed about it. I am willing to listen to your idea, Marshal Diaz."

Diaz smiled appreciatively. "A woman with guts."

Tony silently agreed. It had taken enormous courage to do what she did to get Carter out of the car. That fearlessness was why he'd noticed her in the first place that day he'd met her at the camera store. The owner, in a somewhat patronizing fashion, had suggested a sleek compact camera with a shiny pink case. Willow laughed good-naturedly and pointed to the professional camera bristling with lenses on the very top shelf. "That one, please," she'd said. "Want me to climb up and get it?"

And he found his mind saying the same thing about her. *That one* was the friend he wanted, a strong woman with opinions and plans. A selfish choice on his part, uncharacteristically impulsive. The hurt on her face when she'd learned of his lies would have been enough to send most women packing. But here she was, sitting in the chair, waiting expectantly.

Sheriff Severe nodded. "Willow doesn't surprise me. The Duke clan is a strong bunch, every last one of them."

"All right, here's what I'm thinking." Diaz was standing now, no longer leaning on the desk. "We've got a two-week window until the trial resumes. We need Ron, and if he's got evidence we can use to bolster the DA's case, even better. I want to keep you all here in town."

"But we'd be sitting ducks..." Tony started.

"No. Klee doesn't know where you went. He'd assume you'd run, not hunker down." She looked to Tony.

Willow raised an eyebrow. "Hang on. Let's not sugarcoat this. You want Tony to stay local because you're hoping Ron will come back for his kids, don't you?"

Diaz showed a hint of surprise that Willow had been thinking along the same lines she had.

He remembered his uncle Gino's words. *If you don't cut your brother out of your life, he'll destroy you.* Why hadn't he listened long ago? "Ron loves Bee and Carter. We're essentially bait to get him to return," he said bitterly.

"I wouldn't put it that way. We'll honor our WITSEC commitment. If you want, we'll set you up with a new identity again no questions asked, but once the trial's over, it will be up to you to maintain it with no more interference from the marshals." She paused. "Or you could keep this identity. It's possible Gaudy doesn't know all the particulars of your living details. His guy Klee might have stumbled onto you because he was following Ron."

Tony's hands fisted. "But now he knows that I'm caring for the children."

"Yeah. They complicate things." She hoisted a brow. "Doesn't seem to me like you have much of a chance at a normal life for you or the kids unless we put Gaudy away. Our best shot at that is finding Ron, keeping him alive long enough to testify and convincing him to hand us whatever he's stolen."

"And lure him back using the children," Willow said with some acid.

She shrugged. "You say using. I say capital-
izing on an opportunity."

Tony flashed back on the angry phone conversation with his brother.

You have to come back and testify.

*That's not an option. I never should have
agreed in the first place. I've thought it over.
Gaudy will get off thanks to his fancy lawyers
and come after me later. I gotta get out of the
country, but he's going to bankroll our escape.*

*No, Ron. You're talking nonsense. Go to
the cops. Testify, then take back your kids
and start a new life in WITSEC.* He'd known
before he'd even finished that Ron would not
choose that option.

Tony blinked back to the present. "He told
me before the shooter showed up at the airstrip,
that he was going to retrieve a flash drive and
blackmail Gaudy with it. He'd sent it somewhere for safety before the trial. I was telling
him he was being irrational to try and put the
squeeze on a man who was already out to get
him." He groaned. "My brother is my only sibling, and he's had it tough, but the guy sabo-
tages himself at every turn. This time, he's
sabotaged the rest of us too."

Willow's brow was bunched in thought.
"Back to the plan. You're suggesting that Tony,

the kids stay here in Furnace Falls so I can help them."

Diaz's look was calculating. "You know the area, the town, the people. You can help keep the kids safe and act as eyes and ears too. To be honest, I'm already pushing things. The only manpower I've got is me and Severe, so I can't watch two places at once."

Willow blinked. "Wait, you mean you actually want me to stay on the same premises?"

"Yep. Let's put all the eggs in one basket and get this thing done. If Klee finds you alone in your apartment, you're in real trouble."

Willow raised her brows at Diaz. "Don't try to scare me into helping. I don't think Klee saw me clearly enough to identify me."

"You sure about that?"

Willow resisted the urge to squirm. "Not completely."

Tony gulped.

Diaz smiled. "See? All of you together, hiding in plain sight. The perfect plan," Diaz said with a grin. "It's the only way for us to keep everyone safe. It's not like I'm asking you go get married or something."

"Good," Willow snapped, cheeks flushing pink.

Tony finally recovered his powers of speech.

"What's your real motive here, Diaz? Are you more interested in protecting us or catching Ron?"

Diaz lifted a careless shoulder. "Both. Don't forget, Tony, we're still your best option at surviving this. We put you up someplace in Furnace Falls under Severe's watchful eye, separate living areas etc., of course. Two weeks is all we need to get Ron or the trial is a bust anyway. Willow provides extra protection for the children because she can spot a stranger a mile away, and she's under our protective umbrella too." She shrugged. "There's a place at the airstrip, some unused apartments. Great visibility and easy to secure."

Willow's tone was still incredulous. "I've lived in Furnace Falls all my life," she said. "How am I going to explain moving to the airstrip?"

"Good point," Severe said. "Small town, everybody knows everybody. That's gonna look weird."

Diaz considered that. "Take your family into your confidence then, if you have to, only the closest need to know about it. Hopefully in two weeks we'll have Ron at the trial and we can relocate Tony someplace else with the kids until Gaudy is sentenced."

Willow hugged her arms around herself. "I'm not very good at keeping secrets."

Tony stood. "Willow has done enough. I can't ask her to wade in any deeper."

"I'd say it's your funeral," Diaz said softly, "but there are two little kids sucked into the mess too. Isn't it worth it for their sake?"

"I'll figure it out." Heart in his shoes, he trudged to the door. How exactly would he figure it out? Carter had almost been killed. Sure he could disappear with the kids until Ron enacted his zany plan, but who knew how long that would take? Weeks? A month? What would he do when they needed to go to school? To the doctor? He couldn't keep them under a rock until Ron ran away to Mexico with them. The unfairness of it all swamped him.

"I'll do it," he heard Willow say softly.

He thought he'd misheard, but when he whipped a look at her, she was watching him, the hurt of his lies still nestled in her gaze.

"For two weeks." She added, "For Carter and Bee. I'll live at the airstrip and help you."

And just like that his life was turned upside down again. All he could do was stare.

"One more thing you should know before we get things in motion," Diaz said.

Tony didn't think he had the mental capacity to take in "one more thing" but he stopped.

"We didn't recover Devon Klee's body from the cliff side," she said without missing a beat.

So the hit man was still alive.

And waiting for another chance.

FOUR

Two days later Willow was staring at the faces dearest to her in the world; her brother Austin and his new bride, Pilar; her twin, Levi, and his wife, Mara; and her cousin Beckett. Beckett's wife, Laney, and new baby, Fiona, nicknamed Muffin, were visiting Willow's parents in Florida where they spent spring and summer to avoid the scorching temperatures. Willow had decided to drop the news on everyone at the Hotsprings Hotel, Beckett and Laney's place, since it would be easy to spot any nefarious vehicles in the lot and Beckett's personal cabin was separate from the guests and screened by a privacy fence.

Willow tried to relax as she settled onto a patio chair behind the cabin. The fence did not completely obscure the sprawling Funeral Mountains, majestic in the desert air. The evening brought a breeze, which dropped the temperature into the nineties, along with the chatter of guests enjoying the fire pits and the swimming pool.

From here, it was a stone's throw to Levi and Mara's Rocking Horse Ranch, which they co-owned with Mara's brother, Seth. Horses, brothers, cousins and the most incredible landscape in the world. Furnace Falls had it all if you could stand the life-threatening summer heat.

Tony perched uneasily on the chair next to her. Carter and Bee were lying down on the sofa inside the cabin, sound asleep after Pilar plied them with grilled cheese sandwiches and Mara followed up with cookies from the bakery. Beckett had brought a spare baby monitor which was hooked up on a side table, Tony carrying the receiver. It looked odd in his hands, as if it didn't belong there.

After a deep breath, Willow plunged into her story. She finished up her explanation with, "So I'm going to hole up at the airstrip for a few weeks."

Her words might as well have been meteors crash-landing onto parched desert ground. She counted off the seconds in her head as she waited for the aftershock. Levi, her quiet twin, had that look he got when he encountered someone mistreating a horse, deep-seated fury. He leaped to his feet. "You have got to be kidding."

Austin was standing now too. The shoulder he'd ruined in a climbing accident hitched an inch or so lower than his other. His blond hair gleamed in the firelight, matching the outrage kindling in his eyes. After a false start, he finally got it out. "This isn't right."

"That's putting it mildly," Levi snarled. "There is no way this is going to happen," he fired off at Tony. "No way, you understand me?"

Beckett, the eldest of the Dukes at the gathering, cleared his throat. Rubbing a hand over his dark beard he fixed Tony with a look.

"What Levi means is…you lied to Willow," he said simply.

Tony sighed. "Yes. I had to lie about our identity. The children…"

"No," Levi snapped. "This isn't about the children. You did it because you needed help, so you took advantage of her good nature, and now you've dragged her into a mess."

Tony looked pained. "It isn't what I meant to happen."

"Hardly matters what you meant," Levi said. "Damage done. Now get out of her life."

Mara stepped closer and put a hand on his

wrist, but she didn't interrupt. Levi spoke rarely, but when he did, everybody listened.

"I understand," Tony said, after a long pause. He got to his feet. "I know it doesn't mean much, but I am truly sorry for what's happened." He looked helplessly around the small patio. "This was a bad idea."

"Real bad," Austin echoed. "What kind of a man are you to treat your lady like that?"

"Stop," Willow said, waving them all back down, warm with mortification. "Tony and I weren't dating. It wasn't like he was trying to rope me into a relationship. We are friends. Nothing more. I chose to help him."

Levi glowered. "You were friends with a guy who knowingly made you a target without your permission. In my book that's no kind of friend."

"Levi, I've already accepted the assignment, so to speak. Two weeks, I can live with."

"Unless this hit man or his boss finds you," Austin put in. "Change your mind. Let Tony find someone else to manipulate."

Tony's hands fisted and she could hear his shallow breaths. "They're right," he said. "This plan isn't going to work. I'll get the kids and go."

Willow ignored him, still eyeing her brothers. "Tony doesn't have anyone else, and I'm doing this for the children."

Levi glowered. "Don't you see he's using them to get your help?"

Willow glared right back. "He doesn't have to use them. I care about Carter and Bee, and I am going to be there for them."

"Are you sure this isn't a way to prove something to yourself?" Levi said.

"Don't, Levi," Mara said softly.

But it was too late. Willow felt the flood of shame and uncertainty rolling back in. Were her actions truly set in motion by the ongoing ripples of that betrayal the year before? "This situation has nothing to do with Brad," she said through clenched teeth. Brad, the friend she'd trusted implicitly, dated a few times, and even considered making a business partner, until he stole her work and wrecked her self-confidence. Was this need to help Tony some strange way to prove to herself that she could trust her own judgment again? "He needs help with the children and another set of eyes." She paused before delivering the next words. "There is also the possibility that Klee knows who I am."

Levi blew out a breath. "This gets better and better. You don't need police protection. We will take care of you."

"Yeah? Who is going to run your ranch? Seth can't do it alone." She looked at Austin. "And you have a wife now and a shop to run. Beckett has the hotel. You all can't drop everything to babysit me."

"But—" Levi started.

She stared him down. "If you can figure out a better way to give us all a chance at getting our lives back, I'm listening."

Silence, except for the crackle of the fire.

She lifted her chin in triumph. "That's what we came up with too, nothing. The only way to save the kids is to convict Gaudy, and that means waiting for Ron to show up and convincing him to testify. We'll all be under the marshals' protection until then. See, little brother?" Her twin was two minutes younger, and she never let him forget it. "I'm using my head, not just my untrustworthy heart." Her bitter tone made him flinch.

"Aww, sis," he said, rubbing his chin. "I didn't mean…"

But she didn't want to hear his apology just then. "I know what I'm doing."

"Can I ask a question?" Pilar's hair had almost gone back to its natural blond since she no longer had to hide her identity. It was plaited into a loose braid. She toyed nervously with the end. "If I understood everything, the marshals are suggesting you live in Furnace Falls instead of moving you elsewhere for their own purposes, right? It's to their benefit that Tony and the kids stay close?"

"Yes." Tony eyed the angry men staring back at him over the flames. "Ron still has my cell phone number and he'll have to come to me to get the kids or tell me where he is so I can deliver them. We are a useful part of the game, like checkers. It's been unfair from the start, but at least before I thought it was temporary, that Gaudy would go to prison. Then Ron ran away during the postponement. I figured Gaudy had accomplished his mission. I thought it was over."

"Bonehead move," Austin said.

"Wouldn't be my first." Tony straightened. "I don't expect you to sympathize. I left my life behind, everything I worked for, but I never intended to drag anyone else into the drama."

"I understand what it feels like to live in hiding," Pilar said quietly. Austin slung an arm around her. Their marriage had been interrupted by a killer two months before, and they'd only recently put it all behind them. Willow still caught Pilar's nervous glances sometimes when someone would approach unexpectedly. Austin squeezed her close.

"All over now," he murmured.

Tony gave Pilar an appreciative nod. "Like I said, I shouldn't have invited Willow into my life."

Willow, the mistake. Willow tried for a laugh. "My brothers know I never wait for an invitation." The joke fell flat.

Levi folded his arms. "Cry me a river, Tony. You did drag her in, no matter what you say. I'm sorry about your life being upended, but you had no right to do the same to our sister."

Austin mirrored Levi's expression, the two standing there like two immovable boulders, flanked by their wives.

"Guys," Willow said, "I'm a grown woman and you know me well enough to understand that I make my own choices. I've made this one. I'm not asking for your blessing, only for some understanding, but I'll do without if I have to."

Tony cleared his throat and locked gazes with her. "Your brothers are right. This is too much to risk, too much to ask."

She shook her head. "Most of the time they are, but on this occasion, they are letting protectiveness cause them to forget they aren't my bosses."

A rustle came over the baby monitor, startling Tony. He pulled the gadget from his pocket. "I'll go check on the kids."

When Tony went inside the house, Willow sagged, trying to hide the soreness from the scrapes and bruises she'd acquired pulling Carter from the sedan. How close they'd come to losing him. Were it not for Tony, she'd have gone over the cliff too. Then again, were it not for Tony, she wouldn't have been there in the first place.

She didn't regret it, she realized. God used her to help Carter and that was enough. She'd become so insular after Brad's betrayal, only investing care and attention on her family, the safe people. And then Tony had entered the picture and suddenly she stepped out of the sheltering nest she'd made to extend a helping hand.

And look where that got you.

When Levi started in again, she held up a palm. "We're not going to agree on my choice, okay? Let's switch the topic to accommodations. The marshal said we'll be living in the old apartment at the airfield. Easy to spot intruders, and Tony's a pilot so it makes sense. How bad are they?"

Austin shrugged. "Dusty, mostly. No air-conditioning, just a swamp cooler, but during the day the lower level gets some relief from the cool air that comes up from the tunnel."

Levi rolled his eyes. "Great. Tunnels. And

how is all this going to be secured from the Dark Web Master?"

Willow arched an eyebrow. "Let's not get carried away. Gaudy's a human criminal, not Darth Vader."

Beckett looked like he'd swallowed something poisonous.

"What?" she demanded. "Now's the time to say whatever's on your mind."

Beckett clasped his thick fingers together. "I met some people while I was in prison."

Beckett never spoke of his false imprisonment. She tried not to look too startled.

"I heard the talk from the inmates who did their wheeling and dealing on the dark web. A few were in after getting busted by some undercover FBI agents, but for the most part, bad guys know how to navigate the web and escape detection. Most of all, they know that squealing about what goes on there gets you real dead, real fast. I never heard Gaudy's name, but they referred to someone called the Maestro." He grimaced.

Willow's mind spun. "I did some research last night. In the coverage of Gaudy's pretrial, that same nickname came up."

Levi frowned. "I wonder about the trial postponement. Did Diaz say anything about threats to the judge?"

Her nerves shrank. "No, but I'm sure she's not telling us everything."

"After you called me to arrange this meeting, I called Jude," Beckett said. "He told me the judge said she had to tend to her ailing mother."

"A lie?" Levi asked.

"Not totally. Her mother was ailing, recovering from a surgery. Jude's thought was that there was some sort of hint left at the hospital about what would happen to her vulnerable mother if she presided over the trial. She hasn't made it official, but Jude said he wouldn't be surprised if she recused herself and another judge was appointed to go forward with the case. Could be Ron believes the judge was pressured too, and that pushed him to bolt."

"And nothing could be tied to Gaudy? No hint of intimidation?" Austin said.

Beckett nodded. "Gaudy didn't get his hands dirty, you see. He has puppets to do that on his behalf for a substantial sum. That's why he's called the Maestro."

"And Diaz kept this from us." Willow swallowed the fear and tipped her chin to meet her cousin's gaze. "All the more reason I need to help Tony. He's all those children have got right now."

Resignation crept across her brothers' faces, and she relaxed a fraction.

"All right," Levi said wearily. "If we can't talk you out of this, we'll try to help you as much as we can."

At least she'd won the battle of the Dukes. Now on to the war with Gaudy. She embraced Levi. He hugged her fiercely. "I hope you know what you're doing."

Austin was next and he whispered in her ear, "Why can't I have a nice boring sister who knits tea cozies and stuff?"

She laughed and kissed him. "I often wonder the same thing about my brothers."

She kissed Beckett on the cheek too. "Dukes for the win," she crowed. "I'm going to ask Tony when he wants to leave for the apartment."

"Right behind you," Mara said. She tucked Willow's arm in hers. "I'm not a kid expert, but I'm getting better at it after spending time with my nephew. I'm in."

Willow felt a swell of gratitude. She didn't know her other sister-in-law quite as well, but her affection for Mara was cemented the moment she realized how deeply Mara loved Levi, accepting him for the quiet, unassuming cowboy he was and always would be. And the way

Mara had never given up searching for her lost sister was an example Willow held on to.

They tiptoed inside the back door so as not to wake the children. The interior was cool and still. Willow's senses tingled. There was something off. The quiet, she realized, no static of the baby monitor, or soft rustling of the children, no squeak of the rocking chair Laney used to soothe her own little angel.

Worry flashed through her as she smacked on the light switch. Her heart dropped. The room was empty. Moo Moo, Bee's toy, lay on the floor, forlorn.

Levi exhaled behind her. "He took off."

A chill of fear trickled across her nerves. She whirled on her heel. "Levi, if you tell me this is for the better, I will sock you."

"Wasn't gonna say that."

"Good," she said, snatching up the toy. "Because you're going to help me find them."

Levi shot a pleading look at Austin.

"They don't want to be found, Willow," Austin said. "They left for good reasons."

Frantic energy filled her as she thrust the stuffed cow at them. "If they choose to go it alone, so be it, but Bee isn't going to lose her lovey toy. Those two kids have had to part with their father, their home, and now they're going on the run to some faraway place where they'll have to learn a whole new set of lies to stay alive." Her vision blurred until she blinked away the sudden moisture. "Bee is going to get Moo Moo back if I have to search every square inch of this desert to find them." She realized she'd practically shouted.

Her brothers stared at each other and then at her.

"All right," Austin said, after a breath. "Moo Moo goes back to Bee, but if Tony wants to continue on alone, you let him. Agreed?"

"Agreed," she said. At least she would know that she'd tried her best. "They had a half hour head start. Tony had arrived at the Hotsprings in his white Jetta, which was missing from the hotel parking lot when they checked."

"He'd take 95 South. Head to Las Vegas. Catch a flight somewhere."

"Not a flight, not yet," Willow said. "I think he'll try to get back to his place in Spring Town, it's about fifteen minutes outside of Las Vegas."

Levi raised an eyebrow as they took in the quiet desert road winding away into the darkness. "Why would he do that? Way too risky."

"When the police were interviewing us, he said he had passports for the kids, fake ones, with the Ortega name on them that the marshals provided. They're at his house."

"Ah," Mara said. "He can't fly the kids out of the country without them."

"That's where he's headed, I'm sure," Willow said.

"Do we call the police?" Beckett asked.

"He's chosen not to go the way the marshals suggested," Austin said. "That's not a crime. I say we track him down, deliver the cow and see what happens."

Levi sighed. "You realize that sounds like the worst idea ever."

Austin laughed. "Or the perfect Duke plan." He nuzzled his wife's neck before he spoke again. "Can you and Mara see if you can get in touch with Jude? He might have some unofficial suggestions."

Mara's eyebrows crimped. "Are we womenfolk being left behind?"

Levi smiled. "Purely for practical reasons. Even with the extra row of seats, my truck will be crowded with three and a seat for my rifle. Back soon."

"I am passed over in favor of a rifle," Mara grumped, but there was an undercurrent of concern in her tone. "Be safe."

Willow climbed into the passenger seat and Levi took the wheel. Austin folded his six-foot frame into the backseat.

Without another word, they drove out of

Furnace Falls onto highway 95, a smooth ribbon of road cutting through the desert terrain.

Willow looked up at the stars. Her nighttime photography tours were spent marveling at the sheer magnitude of the Mojave, washed in wonder and steeped in starlight. Now it felt like an endless void into which two frightened children were running with their desperate uncle.

Tony, where are you?

Tony tried to restore his breathing to a regular rhythm as he stared at the home he'd rented in Spring Town. The risk had to be taken. Had it only been two days before when he'd been laughing with Willow, watching Bee press kisses on Moo Moo?

Had he felt the tingle of his conscious telling him that he was wrong, that they were worlds away from being a regular family? The whole notion of having a normal friendship was a fantasy, born of his loneliness and bad decision-making. Selfish.

He unbuckled his seat belt. Now wasn't the time. He had to focus. If Gaudy was sending Klee after them, he had to be prepared to fly the kids out of state or even out of the country if it came to that. The marshal's plan to trap his brother wasn't going to work anyway, and it had resulted in too many outsiders being dragged into his dangerous world.

He rubbed his eyes, which were stinging with fatigue. Bee had cried so hard on the drive after she'd realized Moo Moo was missing that Tony's head was still throbbing. How could toddler lungs attain such a decibel level? And why hadn't he thought to grab the ridiculous toy when he'd whisked them from the cabin?

Because you're not dad material.

No, I'm not, he felt like shouting aloud. *I didn't sign up for this.*

Yet here he was, risking everything. Again. The house was dark, only a slight gleam from the covered porch. The papers were inside an envelope, buried under a stack of folded towels in the linen closet.

The documents were another piece in the puzzle of lies and if he'd known what was going to happen at the airstrip, what his brother was intending, he might have fled the country with the kids already. But even that distance probably wasn't enough to protect them from Gaudy, the Maestro. *Thanks a lot, Ron.* Tony had hardly been able to keep his rage inside when Ron appeared there, sweating with fear, expression desperate.

I'm going to make Gaudy pay.

What do you mean, Ron? Give the cops

whatever you have and testify. You're gonna get us killed.

But Ron had responded, the same look on his face their father, Carl, had whenever he'd announced his latest get rich scheme. Which is why their dad was in jail for embezzlement and likely to stay there. His brother was going to wind up in an early grave. The question was how many people would he take with him?

Tony left the Jetta in the deep shadow of a truck parked along the street. Was the house being watched by Devon Klee, or another of Gaudy's men? He would not risk staying long enough to pack up belongings, just time for grabbing the documents and Carter's favorite dinosaur and something soft for Bee to take the place of Moo Moo. If things seemed safe, he'd also snatch the bundle of cash he'd stowed in an empty paint can. If Gaudy really was the techno genius he was purported to be, it would be best not to leave a digital money trail. He gave himself five minutes.

Everything was quiet, except for the trilling of some night insect.

Surveying the surroundings came natural to him, after his forest service work. For a while, he'd been a lead plane operator. His job was to fly into any situation and scope out an escape route for the big tankers that would drop the fire retardant. Man, how he'd loved that job. How he'd worked himself to the bone to get it, not an easy task with an incarcerated single father.

"You survive in spite of your family," Uncle Gino said one time as he cleaned his service revolver. "Not because of them." Another gem from Gino, who'd taught him all kinds of lessons, mostly the hard and unforgiving ones.

Having decided the best entrance and escape route would be through the garage, Tony zipped his dark jacket up to his chin in spite of the fact that the evening was still warm and pulled on a black baseball cap before he hurried across the street. *Five minutes*, he repeated. Tops. In and out, and on the road.

To where? He unlocked the side gate and quickly closed it behind him. Some small town where no one knew them? He couldn't even change his cell number or Ron would have no way of finding him.

The only choice was to start over and hide until Gaudy lost interest or the unlikely event that his brother got a dose of common sense, dropped his blackmail idea and decided to testify. Tony would never see Willow again, that was a given. Just as well, he told himself grimly.

The side garage door opened with a squeal

as he removed his key from the lock. Inside he listened again, the air hot and scented with the faint odor of gasoline and mildew. He was about to activate his cell phone light when the overhead bulb flicked on, momentarily blinding him.

He flinched as Klee swam into view, standing by the light switch, a knife in his hand. His curls were oily black in the gloom.

"Remember me?" the hit man said.

Tony's brain tumbled thought after thought. How was he going to get out of this one?

"Devon Klee."

Klee twisted his lips. "Everyone calls me Klee. I don't like the name Devon. Sounds like some prep school snot." He held up an envelope. "Came for this, didn't you?"

Tony knew with a sickening feeling what Klee was holding. His mouth was sand dry.

Klee tucked the envelope into the pocket of his windbreaker. "Where are they?"

"Who?"

He pursed his thick lips. "The kids."

"Somewhere safe."

Klee cocked his head. "Huh. Maybe you're smarter than I thought."

"Thanks."

"But I'll find them anyway."

"It'll take a while. Do you have time to spare? Gaudy's not a patient man, right?"

Klee considered the question. "I'll hurt you until you tell me," he said, matter-of-factly.

Tony was still dreaming up plans and discarding them. He had no weapon, only his cell phone.

He could try for the door to the house. Lock himself in and call for help.

Klee moved three steps to his right, effectively blocking that route.

Tony considered what he knew about knife fights. Not much, except that there were very few scenarios in which an unarmed man didn't get himself cut or worse. But Uncle Gino had taught him a few things. He needed more time to think.

"You've worked for Gaudy a long time?" Tony asked.

Klee nodded. "Yeah, and he wants you dead, but I get to keep the kid."

Tony's mouth dropped open. "What?"

"The boy, the one I snatched from the airstrip. I'm retiring soon and I want a son around to go fishing with. Go to baseball games and stuff like that."

Tony regathered his powers of speech. "Kids aren't like suitcases. You can't grab the one you want."

Klee laughed. "Suitcases. Good one. He's young. He'll forget about you and Ron. I'll be his dad. He's gonna call me Pops, like I called my dad."

Tony felt like he was in the middle of a non-sensical nightmare.

"Don't want a girl. Too much trouble, and they always need expensive stuff. The boy, I'll take him. Where is he?"

Tony was probably the worst uncle turned father ever. Clueless, frustrated, with no knowledge about raising kids. Not surprising, with his family history. But at Klee's revelation, something switched on inside of Tony. Fear turned to granite-hard determination. Bad father or not, he wasn't talking. He would die before he told Klee anything about the children. But he wasn't dead quite yet. He glanced around.

Why did he have to keep such a neat garage? There was not one errant tool or rake lying nearby, only organized cupboards that offered no help. All he had was his phone.

A buzzing sounded and Klee pulled out his own cell, without taking his eyes off Tony. He grinned and flicked on the speaker button.

"Hello, Tony," came a man's voice, slightly nasal. "This is Otto Gaudy."

Tony didn't answer.

"Tony? Are you there?" Gaudy asked after a moment.

"Yes," he said, amazed that his voice sounded rock-solid. "I'm here. What do you want?"

"All right. Let me be clear and to the point. I am going to punish your brother and he will never testify. That is unnegotiable. You, I don't care about. Klee is there to take the boy, which will force Ron out into the open. Klee will get me what I want, he always does, but it would be faster if you'd cooperate. The girl can stay with you. Better some than none, and so much less pain."

Tony was momentarily speechless. "Family isn't your thing, I take it," he managed. *You monster.*

"You err. As a matter of fact, this is part of the issue. Family is everything, and my wife, Eugenia, betrayed me with your *brother*." He drew out the last word as if he was speaking to an imbecile. "Another reason why he will die publicly, and in the most painful way Klee can think of."

"I've already got an idea about that." Klee nodded.

"You're done, Tony," Gaudy said. "The only thing you can influence here is time."

Tony wrestled with a massive wave of fury. He wasn't done. He might be flying on fumes without a landing zone in sight, but things were far from over. Keeping his face impassive, he waited for his chance.

"Klee?" Gaudy asked sharply. "Is he listening to me?"

The sharp tone drew Klee's attention to his phone for a scant second.

It was all Tony needed. Praying something remained from his high school pitching days, he lobbed his phone at the overhead light. The bulb smashed with a satisfying crunch, and the garage went dark.

FIVE

"I don't see Tony's car." Willow scanned the dark, narrow street. Tony's rented house faced an open space with a creek, dry now. Three houses only on this block, all quiet, everyone tucked in for the night. "I was certain he'd have come back, but maybe I was wrong."

She bit back a sigh. No surprise there. She'd been wrong about everything where Tony was concerned. He wasn't a friend, and most of what he'd told her were outright lies. She felt a pain under her rib cage and breathed it away. Where had her ability to trust her instincts gone?

"Could be he stopped somewhere along the way and we beat him here," Austin mused. "Beckett says with a kiddo you never get anywhere when you think you will. I'm going to take a look."

He got out of the truck, Levi following. Willow didn't even speak, merely handed Levi his rifle. She'd have to argue to accompany them, and it would be pointless anyway, three of them wandering around in the dark. Always have backup, Jude drilled into them all, so she'd assume that role. "I'll keep texting Tony." She climbed into the driver's seat so she could plug in her phone if it went dead.

Where are you? Are you and the kids okay? she texted.

No reply.

Sadness crept up from her belly, engulfing her. She'd likely seen Tony and the kids for the last time. They'd disappeared. Too soon. At least her brothers would be pleased that Tony was out of her life.

Crunch. She stiffened. The sound was almost inaudible and she would have missed it if the street had been noisier. She turned the key in the ignition and rolled down the window. Her pulse thudded. What had she heard?

The shout came next, a deep baritone, charged with adrenaline. Her brothers? She readied her phone to call for the police, fingers clammy. Should she? Shouldn't she? A figure emerged from the shadow-soaked lawn and ran into the driveway. Dark, unidentifiable until he sprinted into a weak gleam from a mounted light. One of her brothers? No, athletic shoes meant it wasn't Levi and the hair was dark, not Austin's blond. Tony.

He stopped and turned as someone appeared behind him, from the direction of the side yard. This time she didn't need to guess. The burly Devon Klee charged after Tony, his knife glinting silver. Her nerves iced over.

Tony stumbled, went down to one knee. He wasn't going to outrun Klee. More sounds indicated Levi and Austin were not far behind, in danger, all three of them.

Without a second thought she cranked on the engine, pulled the truck around to face the house and switched on the headlights. Klee threw up an arm to shield his eyes as Tony tried to right himself. Willow watched in horror as Klee pulled back his arm. She knew what was next—her brothers had spent summers practicing their knife throws when they were kids.

With the heel of her hand, she slammed on the horn. The blare tore apart the quiet. Klee was still moving. There was only one choice available, so she stomped on the gas pedal, careening up the driveway, praying she did not hit Tony or her brothers. The house loomed close, closer. Her move came too late. Klee's shoulder arced forward, momentum carrying the blade. The knife flew through the night and she lost track of it. Tony dropped out of sight. Panicked, she practically stood on the brakes, the vehicle screeching as it slowed. Where was Klee? Had his knife found its mark? She could not see Tony either.

Levi appeared from the backyard, rifle on his shoulder as the bumper of the truck kissed the garage door and she held the wheel, rigid and panting. Their eyes connected for a moment. They'd never needed more than a look to communicate. She was unhurt. Reassured, Levi sprinted around the truck and took off running, no doubt in pursuit of Klee, who had disappeared. Austin jogged over.

She slammed open the truck door and tumbled out, running for Tony. Bloody visions crowded her brain as she ran to him. Austin was crouched down next to Tony.

"Tony?" She had to push the words out of her dry mouth.

"If you were two inches taller, you'd be having a really bad day," Austin said to Tony.

Her gaze traveled up the wooden garage door. About the location where Tony's head would have been, was a knife embedded to the hilt.

Tony straightened and got to his feet. "Yeah." He was breathing hard. "At least my ducking reflexes are still on par."

Willow's own heartbeat had not slowed one iota as Levi reappeared.

"Lost him."

"Not surprised," Austin said. "Guy's a pro."

"He was waiting here for me," Tony said.

Levi rested his rifle over his shoulder. "How'd you get away?"

Tony didn't seem to hear. He was staring in the direction Klee had fled. "He's got the passports for the kids. And he said he's going to take Carter to raise as his son."

"What?" Willow felt sick. Levi and Austin shared similar expressions of disgust.

"I'll call Marshal Diaz right now," she said.

"Wait on that," Tony said, "until I get the kids."

She gaped. "I thought they were in the house. Where are they?"

"About an hour from here, safe. I figured if Klee was planning an ambush, I'd better be prepared." He wiped a palm over his weary face and cocked his chin at Willow and her brothers. "Why'd you come? I'm grateful, but I didn't think you'd tail us."

Willow pulled the toy from her pocket. "Bee needs Moo Moo and you need a place to hide and a friend to watch your back." Her tone was forceful and clear. "I hope you're not going to argue, after what's happened here."

He exhaled, hands on hips. Desperation enhanced his age, pushing him past his thirty-five years. "There's too much at risk," he said after a long pause. "I can't…"

Willow jammed Moo back into her pocket. "You're right. There's too much to risk, Bee and Carter, especially now that this thug has decided he's going to kidnap Carter for himself. You need help and you're going to have to take it whether you like it or not."

She waited to see how her pronouncement would be received. Her brothers always told her she was too impulsive, and they'd been right about Brad, so right. But Tony wasn't Brad and she knew deep down God had put her in Tony's path to help him. Crickets chirped from their hidden places, ticking off the silence with their rhythmical beats. Still Tony hesitated.

Austin quirked a brow. "Listen man, I don't like the plan either, but I know that tone of Willow's so you might as well get in the truck and we'll go pick up the kids."

Tony's glance swiveled to Levi.

He shrugged. "Different game now. No one's gonna abduct a child on my watch. We'll help protect you as best we can, so you can get on your way." His last words were flinty. Tony wasn't forgiven; Levi had made that clear. It was a business arrangement only. *Don't worry, Levi. This isn't a love thing. I learned my lesson about trusting liars.* A friend helping a friend.

"Klee is probably in the area, so we'd better get out of here ASAP," Austin said. "And he knows your car, Tony, so you'll be better off leaving it."

Tony quickly retrieved the car seats from his vehicle, stowing them in the back of the truck before they climbed in. Austin held Levi's rifle so Tony could squeeze himself into the jump seat adjacent to hers. Willow's phone buzzed. "It's Diaz. She wants to talk." She frowned. "How could she have heard what happened already? We didn't even call the police yet."

Tony shook his head. "Not talking to her until I get the kids."

Willow cocked her head. "You don't trust her?"

Tony stared at his clasped hands. "I don't trust anybody. Gaudy can buy whatever and whomever he wants...even marshals."

Even marshals.

If Diaz or Severe, or someone else working with them was feeding information to Gaudy, then Furnace Falls would not be the safe haven they needed. Could they be bringing the trouble right to her family's lap?

She swallowed hard. Would Furnace Falls be a shelter or a snare?

Austin looked in the rearview at him. "Well, Tony, you're in for more help that you know what to do with. You request one Duke, you get them all."

Willow giggled. "It's okay. That's not as scary as it sounds." She reached for Tony's hand and squeezed it. She wanted to tell him with the gesture that he wasn't alone. His fingers were cold and though he looked startled, he squeezed back.

"Thank you," he said quietly. "You bought me a few seconds with the truck thing. I had enough time to duck." A faint smile touched his lips, a small scar visible just at the corner of his mouth. For one moment, he pressed her hand to his cheek. Accepting the offer of help? Grateful for her family's intervention?

The touch and the beginning of trust it represented made something flutter inside her until she pushed it down. *Be careful, Willow. Don't expect him to trust you when you can't reciprocate.* He let go and they sank into silence as Levi drove the route Tony gave him, checking for any signs that someone was following.

And she knew there would be eventually.

Klee, Gaudy or others he employed. Tony told him what Gaudy had said.

"You're done, Tony."

And maybe he would have been at their mercy if he was alone, without allies. But the Maestro hadn't counted on one thing...he'd never met the Duke family.

Chin up she looked out the front window into the night.

Tony felt that horrible spiraling sensation that indicated the threads of his life were once again sliding from his grasp. *Lord...* he started. So many thoughts tumbled through him that he couldn't even rustle up a proper prayer. Instead he settled on, *Thank You.*

A thank-you that he had sense enough not to bring the children with him.

That the Dukes had arrived.

That Willow had seen fit to follow his trail in spite of all the trouble he'd caused her.

He realized he was staring at her as they drove the last few miles. The strawberry blond tint of her hair didn't show in the darkness, nor the gray-blue of her eyes which were not as intensely hued as her brothers, but even more vivid somehow. Scattered across her nose was a trail of freckles that she didn't bother to hide with any cosmetics. She attracted him, he had to admit, but not because of a picturesque face. There was a freshness about her, like a delicious cool breeze on a stifling desert day. Which is why he'd wanted to become her friend, to draw alongside that positive spirit somehow.

Which is why her life is now a mess, he reminded himself.

He brought his wanderings to heel. "It's a few blocks down, on the left," he told Levi. "If you want to park here and wait, I'll go get them."

"I'll help," Willow said.

"Then I'm going as backup," Austin said. "Levi, can be our eyes outside. Text me if we've got company."

"Text me too," Tony said, wiggling his phone, which had a crack from when he'd thrown it, but was still functional.

"Me three," Willow said as they got out. They exchanged cell numbers.

"Keep your head on a swivel," Austin told his brother.

Levi grimaced. "Please, if I can track a missing horse across fifty acres, I can spot a human sneaking up the front. You watch the back."

Austin saluted. "Will do."

They approached a well-tended ranch-style

home with neat shrubs along the front. Austin held back. "Do they have a dog?"

"Cats," Tony said.

"Then I'm going to go take a quick look over the back fence while you two snag the pint-sized people." He strolled away toward the side yard. "Nosy, but better than being surprised."

"I met Mrs. Finley at the airstrip," Tony said after he rapped a knuckle on the door. "Her husband, Kyle, owns the flight business. She does filing there to help out, and she's raised seven kids while working as a pediatric nurse. She babysat for me a few times and I trust her completely." He wasn't sure why he felt the need to explain, but he didn't want Willow to think he was a complete loss as a guardian.

A short stocky lady with a chic silver bob of hair answered the door. "Hi, Tony. Come on in. Kyle's still at the airstrip, but he'll be home soon."

Tony introduced Willow. They entered a cozy den with a nicely worn sofa and recliner. It was the perfect homey spot, he thought, with pictures on the walls and a massive dining table, the lingering smell of a warm meal. A better place for Bee and Carter than his rental home where they ate at a makeshift table he'd snagged at a garage sale, and many dinners consisted of bowls of cereal. Bee's room was a dull brown color, when it should be pink and have bunnies painted all over or barnyard scenes or something. "I really appreciate your help, Mrs. Finley. Kids give you any problems?"

She waved a hand. "They've been great. Carter ate a nice dinner of elbow macaroni and peas." She quirked an eyebrow. "I wanted to tell you though, I think Bee sounds a little congested, and she didn't have much of an appetite, even for the cookie I bribed her with. Thought I'd mention it, since you have the asthma struggle with her."

Tony hadn't noticed. Another wave of guilt. "I appreciate that. I will certainly keep an eye on it. Don't want her back in the hospital again." That had been one of the scariest moments of his parenting experience before the kidnapping of Carter. Seeing her struggling for each breath left him feeling completely helpless.

Mrs. Finley went on. "But other than that, everything went like clockwork. Bee and Carter settled right down in the guest room after story time. They loved hearing him read."

Tony was turning toward the hallway that led to the guest room when he froze. "Him?"

She pushed her glasses up. "Uh-huh. Your uncle. He sounded thrilled that you'd asked him to help with the babysitting. He's sitting with them now in case they wake up and need anything."

I didn't call my uncle.

Willow's mouth formed into a petrified line.

Tony was already sprinting down the hallway, Willow on his heels. Every nerve in his body was screaming. Klee had gotten there first. Why would Mrs. Finley have trusted the man's word?

No one's fault but yours.

He skidded over the threshold and as he did so an arm slammed into his chest, knocking him over backward. Willow stumbled against the wall behind him. As he scrambled to his feet, she grabbed up a silver candleholder from a shelf and held it up, ready to take a swing.

His assailant stepped into view. "Quiet down. You startled me running down the hallway like that. You're gonna wake the kids and I had to read this ridiculous story about a bunny and his slippers three times already."

Tony sucked in some breaths, trying to get his lungs operating as he looked at the broadchested man with the shaved head and the contrasting bushy eyebrows.

Willow still stood tense as a wire, arm wielding the candle holder. "You get away from those kids," she hissed.

"Willow," Tony started.

"I mean it." She gripped the silver instrument. "I don't know who you are but if you don't leave this room right now I'm going to start swinging."

Tony interrupted before she could make good on her threat. "Willow, this is my uncle Gino."

"Your uncle?" Willow gaped. "Why didn't you tell me you'd invited him?"

"Because I didn't," Tony said.

"Then how did he know where to find the children?"

"That," Tony said, arms folded across his chest, "is exactly the question I was going to ask."

SIX

Willow put down the candlestick, edged around Uncle Gino and checked on the children. They were both sleeping soundly, covers pulled up to their noses.

"Let's hear it, Uncle Gino." Tony sounded both angry and resigned as Willow listened to the explanation.

"Come out here in the hallway," Gino said, beckoning them. "Like I said, I'm not reading that nutty bunny story again if they wake up." With some reluctance, Willow joined them.

"I got a call from a friend, Rocklin Severe," Gino said.

Tony sighed. "Right. Another old cop buddy." He looked at Willow. "Uncle Gino is a retired state trooper. He knows everybody."

"Yes, I do. Severe told me you hadn't arrived at the place they'd arranged and there appeared to have been trouble at your rented house. They assigned a unit to check it out every few hours. I did some sleuthing, called a few people. Local cop friend of mine said he knew of an airstrip where a pilot fitting your description worked. Airstrip owner's wife is a nice grandmotherly type who babysits when called upon." He shrugged. "It was easy from there." Uncle Gino looped his thumbs through the waistband of his jeans. "Anyway, Severe told me you're hiding out with the kids in Furnace Falls and you need some backup. I wasn't surprised. Still trying to clean up your little brother's messes?"

Willow tried to decipher the undercurrent between the two men. Tension? But there was some level of trust, from Tony's reaction. Love? She wasn't certain. She heard Tony's teeth grind together.

"I'm not getting into this with you right now," he said. "The only thing that matters is keeping the kids safe."

Gino added, "And making Ron do the right thing when he shows up."

Tony's eyes narrowed. "Which is what, in your opinion?"

"Hand over whatever blackmail info he thinks he's got, testify against Gaudy. The kids should go into foster care and stay there since Ron will never shake off the target he's put on his back."

"Foster care?" Willow said after a gasp.

"Why so shocked?" Gino said, glancing at her. "Surely you don't think Tony should sacrifice his life raising kids that aren't even his?"

Tony shook his head. "Like you did with us?"

Willow stared from Tony to Gino. What had gone on between these two?

Gino rocked back on his heels. "I stepped in when my loser of a brother messed up. It cost me career advancement, sure, but I didn't resent it because you turned out good, Tony, *you* were worth the effort."

The slight emphasis on the "you" told her that Gino did not feel the same way about Tony's brother. He went on.

"But I see you falling into the same pattern trying to help Ron. You can't save him. He's a lost cause."

Willow glanced past Gino into the darkened room, praying the children were still sleeping soundly.

"Stop," Tony grunted, voice a low growl. "I don't know the right answers at this moment, but I was attacked by Gaudy's man at my rental house so rehashing our family history isn't top on the list right now."

Gino arched a brow. "Yet you didn't call Severe and Diaz?"

"No."

A long moment passed between them. "Why not?" Gino asked.

Tony didn't answer.

"You think they're on the take?"

Tony waved him off. "I'm leaving with the kids and Willow right now before Gaudy's man catches up."

Gino flicked a glance at Willow. "So she's involved in this too?"

"Yes," Tony said with a sigh. "Diaz wants us to hole up in Furnace Falls. We're in this together."

Together. Willow felt a spot of warmth.

Gino shrugged. "Diaz must have her reasons. Let's roll."

"I don't need your help."

Gino laughed. "Uh-huh. See how easily I got access to the children? Strolled right on in. You need me, son, even if you don't want to admit it."

Tony waved a hand. "I don't have time for this now. The clock is ticking."

"I'll pack up their things," Willow said, happy to be able to escape the tension.

Willow saw Gino catch Tony's arm. "Best thing is to give them to social services. They'd be safest and well cared for."

Social services? What kind of a man was

this uncle? Willow thought as she scooped Bee's sweatshirt and Carter's storybook into a grocery bag. It was a pitiful collection of things, symbolic of the desperate life they'd been living. At least Bee would have Moo Moo back.

Things would be better in Furnace Falls if Gino didn't change Tony's plans. Mara and Pilar would be thrilled to supply the two children with everything they needed. Her mind was spinning with plans when Gino finished.

"You know you can't pull this off alone," he said.

Willow glared. "He's not alone."

Gino laughed and said to Tony, "The little woman with the candlestick is your bodyguard too?"

Tony started to speak but Willow beat him to it.

Cheeks flaming, she marched over and tipped her chin to look at Gino dead-on. "You don't know me well, sir, but I can tell you that I'm a lot more than a 'little woman' and if you don't respect me because I'm female, I've got a family of hardheaded brothers and cousins who will be pleased as punch to chat with you on that topic."

He laughed again. "I admire pluck, and I'm willing to keep an open mind. I'll come along and see what kind of setup you all have in place in Furnace Falls and how I can add value." He doffed an imaginary hat. "If that's okay with you, ma'am."

Though she wanted to tell him exactly what she thought about that idea, she whirled on her heel and returned to the children. She heard Tony's words, simmering with rage as he spoke to Gino in low tones. "Don't talk down to her. She's got the courage of a lion, and Carter and I would be dead if it wasn't for her actions. If you can't respect that, you're not welcome."

There was a pause. Willow's heart beat fast as she pulled back the blankets and scooped Bee into her arms. Tony's words twirled right to her soul, but she dared not look at him.

Gino chuckled again. "Fair enough. I'll meet you in Furnace Falls." He paused and his gaze flicked toward her. "Right now, you aren't in a position to trust anyone. Remember that."

Gino ambled down the hallway, and she heard him strike up a cheerful conversation with Mrs. Finley.

Tony moved toward Carter. "I'm...sorry about that, Willow."

Willow wanted to hold on to her fury, but she couldn't. Tony had stopped it with his defense of her. "No harm done."

"I don't want him in on this, but I'm not certain I can stop him."

"We'll sort it all out later."

Tony squinched his eyes closed.

"Headache?"

"Yeah. Great time for a migraine, huh?"

"Do you have any meds for it?"

He grimaced. "Sure. Back at the house." He waved a hand. "It's fine. I never took them anyway because I didn't want to be groggy around the kids. Let's get going. Can you send Austin and Levi a text before we go out so they don't mistake Gino for an enemy?"

Willow did so as Tony woke Carter and bundled the sleepy child into his sweatshirt, easily lifting his dead weight. She gathered Bee close. When she whimpered, Willow said, "Here's Moo Moo," and tucked the cow under her chin. Bee relaxed immediately, sucking her thumb and clutching the toy. If only adult problems could be solved so easily. She could not resist pressing a kiss to Bee's warm forehead.

Over Bee's shoulder, she caught Tony's gaze.

"Last chance to change your mind," he said with a faltering smile. "I won't hold it against you. The kids and I can go somewhere else. Diaz can't force us."

Last chance to avoid Gaudy's wrath and the abrasive Uncle Gino. Last chance to return to her regular life, without the kids, without Tony, to return to the sole protection of her family.

It was doable. She'd learned to move forward without Brad, hadn't she?

But she wasn't becoming involved in the situation because she wanted a relationship with Tony. It was a "bear one another's burdens" thing. She'd been so hurt by Brad that she'd only been in self-protection mode, focused on family and rebuilding her photography business, nothing outside of that. It felt good to step out for the children.

"I'm in it to win it," she whispered, with a cheeky wink.

His return smile was tender and filled with something that might not be purely gratitude, which sent her nerves into a skitter.

"For the children," she said firmly, carrying Bee from the room.

Even with the third row in Levi's massive truck, it was crowded with two kids and four adults. There was no room to install the car seats so Tony and Willow held the kids as they drove out of town. Their first stop was a rental car agency in Las Vegas.

Willow didn't ask why. She was savvy enough to know that Klee and whoever else Gaudy might have sicced on them had already been given Tony's vehicle description and license plate number. It was smart to leave the vehicle at his rented house. Levi and Austin waited in the truck while he and Willow transferred the kids into the four-seater Toyota with enough room for the car seats.

Willow offered to drive and he sank gratefully into the passenger seat. The space was cramped for his long legs, so he cranked back the seat. When he was sure the kids had dozed off, he called Severe and left a message about what had happened, filling in some details about Klee and which direction he'd run. He did not mention their exact location, vehicle, or how long it would take them to reach Furnace Falls. He had no reason to distrust Severe, except that he'd reached out to Uncle Gino.

For extra protection?

Most likely, but if he was a bad cop, he might be using his connection with Gino to get information for Gaudy. But that didn't make sense. Severe already knew about their plans to stay at the airstrip. What could he possibly need Gino for?

His left temple and eye throbbed with a squeezing pain. He realized he'd gone too long without food, and the stress wasn't helping with the building migraine. He could ask Willow if she had a snack with her, but that would make him look like a child. Hadn't he already put her out enough for one night?

Instead, he tried to calm his tension as they followed the truck over the road that seemed to stretch endlessly through the wild acres of desert. The buildings grew fewer the farther they drove from the Las Vegas area and the closer they got to Death Valley. In spite of himself, he felt his eyelids grow heavy.

"Potty."

The one word of Carter's burst through Tony's doze. He jerked and rubbed his eyes. Where was the nearest facility that was clean enough for a child? The issue had caused him no end of angst over the last four months he'd been caring for the kids. He already had nightmares about how he'd manage when Bee wasn't wearing diapers anymore. He'd invested in a book on potty training, and it had proven so agitating that he'd shoved it in a drawer.

He looked wildly around, trying to place himself. Where could they go? Was it already too late? He had no extra clothes for the boy. Not so much as a clean pair of socks for Carter or an extra diaper for Bee. Irrational panic started up at that single word *potty*. How did normal parents do this on the daily?

"It's okay," Willow said, cutting through his mental muddle. "There's a gas station and mini mart ahead. Pretty decent facilities. I used to stop for coffee when I drove back from baby-sitting for the kids. They've got diapers too." She called over her shoulder. "Can you wait five more minutes, honey?"

Carter nodded.

"And we can get you something to eat too," Willow said to Tony. "And some aspirin."

How had she known he was hungry? For that matter how did she know the right way to handle the kids at every turn? She didn't have kids of her own, and her only niece was a mere three months old. It was that sort of cheerful confidence and optimism that had made him notice her in the first place.

Guilt poked at him. He'd wanted a friend, was that so wrong? Yes, it was, considering he was a danger magnet, resentful about shelving his career, a man who'd lost his way. He didn't have the right to be close to her. *Best remember that, Tony.*

He recalled her brandishing the candlestick at his uncle, and a smile lit his face. Uncle Gino was harsh, but he recognized that Tony was floundering as he slowly sank under the weight of a family he hadn't made, and a path he'd never have chosen. Was he right that Tony should give up on Ron or put the children in foster care? How had he become the decision maker and sole provider for two children who weren't even his? He tried to breathe out the frustration, but it didn't work, not really.

God forgive me, he thought. The children deserved better. Was this wild scheme the way toward providing them a future? If Ron returned and they could put Gaudy away...they had a chance.

Slim, but better than nothing.

At this point, he'd take any chance that was offered, slim or not, as long as Willow and the kids would not be in the bull's-eye again.

Willow parked the car in a side slot at a six-pump gas station. She carried a fussing Bee, while Tony led Carter by the hand. Levi and Austin rolled in next to them.

"How about we keep watch and you bring us two coffees?" Austin asked from the truck. "We work cheap, right?"

Willow noticed Levi didn't join in the joke. He was still simmering, her quiet twin, the kind who would wrestle with thoughts for months before he'd utter them aloud.

I know what I'm doing, Levi.

"Two coffees, one black and yours with triple sugar because Pilar isn't here to remind you about your addiction to sweeteners," she said.

Austin gave her a thumbs-up. "I'll compro-

mise. Two sugars will do. Gotta stay fueled."
His gaze drifted to the darkened parking lot.
"Better make it quick. We're too exposed here,
and my nerves are jumping."

Hers were too.

They hustled inside the large convenience-
type store with facilities in the rear. Tony
headed straight for the family restroom with
Carter who was writhing in discomfort. She
rocked Bee against her, scanning the shelves at
the small section of diapers. Who knew there
were so many size choices? She erred on the
larger size, snagging a handbasket and dropping them in.

Bee was still fussing, pressing her head into
Willow's chest as if protesting against some
toddler injustice. Hungry? Wet diaper? Peevish from being carted from one place to the
next? All of the above? The babysitter's comment about Bee's health concerned Willow,
and she made a mental note to contact Dr.
Howley if the child did not bounce back after
some proper food and sleep.

"It's okay, sweet girl. Just a quick stop and
you can go back to sleep if you want." Willow
continued to joggle Bee with one arm, picking up some vanilla wafers and juice boxes as
well as a premade turkey sandwich for Tony.
At the counter, she slid over the basket while

the clerk fitted four coffees in a cardboard tray. His beard was impressive, a snowy puff that caught Bee's eye.

"Santa," she said, pointing a tiny finger at him. It came out like "aanta" but the clerk got the meaning.

Willow felt herself blushing to her roots. "Oh sorry, sir. It's your beard."

He laughed as he rang up her purchase and Willow had to admit, he certainly sounded jolly.

"Got myself a granddaughter says the same thing. After four grandsons, she's a whole different ballgame, and she's got Papa looped around her tiny pinky. I think I may have something your little girl would like." He winked at Bee and reached under the counter, pulling out two red pinwheels. A look of wonder shown on Bee's face as she accepted it. "Had these leftover from some promotion or another. One for your son too."

"Oh yes." It took her a moment to cover the strangeness of hearing Carter described as her son. The clerk thought she was their mom. "That's so kind. Can't have sister get one and not big brother."

Bee shook the sparkly contraption in excitement.

"That's right. One for each. Nice family."

The clerk's dark eyes riveted on hers and his chuckle died away. "Kids favor your hubby, huh?"

Hubby, right. For some reason she did not think his question was purely idle conversation. She felt a thrill of uncertainty. She tried a smile, determined to avoid outright lying if possible. "They sure don't look like me, do they?"

He studied Bee, who was shaking the pinwheel. It wasn't Willow's imagination. The clerk was flat-out staring now. She wondered if she should leave the items and get out quickly, but how could she communicate to Tony without attracting more attention?

The clerk leaned closer. "You know, it's usually pretty quiet here around this time, mostly people in town. But someone was in here about fifteen minutes ago, a stranger asking questions. A guy wearing sunglasses, at night, if you can imagine. Stocky, with a bruise on his cheekbone like he'd taken a punch recently or something."

She stood frozen. She knew all too well a stocky man who'd recently been in a fight and tumbled over a cliff for that matter. "What... kind of questions?" she forced out.

"Asking if I'd seen a guy with two kids 'bout the same age as yours. Didn't mention a wife, though. Gave me a number to text if I clapped eyes on any family like that. Said there was a hundred bucks in it for me." He leaned forward.

Willow found it hard to breathe.

"A hundred bucks," the clerk said softly. "And all I have to do is send a text. Imagine that."

SEVEN

A rock formed in her stomach and a long moment passed between them.

"I..." Should she offer him more money for his silence? Run? Pretend like she didn't know what he was talking about?

He bagged up her purchases and pushed them at her. "Like I said, I got a granddaughter her age, and I can see that you're taking good care of Sweet Pea here and she trusts you. That kinda thing shows." He reached out a thick finger and twirled the pinwheel for Bee, sending her into delighted giggles. "I don't cotton to strangers offering me bribes to cause trouble. Mr. Sunglasses isn't gonna hear anything from me."

She could hardly squeak out the words as she clutched Bee. "Thank you, sir."

He nodded and handed her a piece of paper. "Here's the number he called from. Dunno if it will help you figure things out, but I don't need it." He stroked his lush beard. "I'd get going quick if I were you, though. No telling where Sunglasses has holed up. He was driving a Dodge. Cost him a bundle to fill that up. I'll keep watching the door while you get her diaper changed in case he's doubled back."

"I don't know how to thank you," she said. "We're in your debt."

He smiled. "It was thanks enough seeing how much Sweet Pea enjoyed the pinwheel. Hurry now, huh? Trouble coming. I can feel it."

As soon as Tony came out, she rushed to him. "Grab the things I bought. The clerk told me someone was here looking for us. It sounds like Klee. I'm going to change Bee as quick as I can, and we have to get away. Can you text my brothers?"

Tony nodded and urged Carter to the counter while she hurried to change Bee. It was probably risky to take the time, but the child's diaper was sodden and with a runny nose already, she didn't want to add to Bee's discomfort.

Tony was waiting by the front door and he escorted her out. Levi was a few paces back, using the car to conceal the fact that he was holding his rifle. Austin had the Toyota engine going and the doors open. Willow waved a thanks once more to the clerk. It was possible he was lying, and he would call the man in sunglasses as soon as she left to collect his hundred dollars, but her instincts told her he was an honest grandpa who meant what he said. She prayed she could trust those instincts again.

Tony strapped Carter into his car seat and she did the same with Bee, who cried until Carter spun the pinwheel for her. Tony drove from the gas station with her brothers trailing them. She called them immediately to give them more details about what the clerk had said.

"Klee must have figured you'd head to the closest rental car agency, and stop for supplies for the young'uns," Levi said. "He's sharp."

"Here." She handed two aspirin to Tony. "It might help your headache."

He took the pills dry, since all four coffees had been hurriedly loaded into Levi's truck, but Austin had tossed the snacks and juice boxes in the backseat. She turned and helped the kids to their provisions while he headed for the freeway. Her heart was still racing. If they hadn't happened upon that grandfatherly clerk…

She swallowed. "Do you think it was Klee wearing the sunglasses?"

"I hope it was," Tony said.

"But..." Then she understood. "If it wasn't, Gaudy's sent more people."

He unwrapped the sandwich and took an unenthusiastic bite, as if his appetite had deserted him. "Only one good bit of news from that. The clerk said he asked about me and the kids, so maybe he's not counting on you being involved."

"I didn't think of that." She grinned. "We're better at this undercover stuff than we thought."

He chuckled. "You've got to be the only woman in the world who could find a bright side in all of this."

"I am one of a kind."

"That you are," he said softly.

She felt her cheeks pink. *He's grateful, that's all.* She remained quiet as they rolled onto the onramp. As one lane split into two, Tony sat straighter. "There's a car behind..." he started, just as her phone rang. She thumbed it on.

"It's Klee, in a Dodge. Got his license plate. No time to get the police. Going to get ahead of you and set up a trap at the next off ramp. Hold tight," Austin said.

Willow fought the urge to turn around and stare at the car approaching them. Her whole body had prickled in gooseflesh. No police backup? What if things went wrong and bullets started flying? With two small children in the rear seat? And her brothers at risk too?

Tony looked outwardly calm but his knuckles were white on the wheel. "Next off ramp is two miles. Gonna keep my speed steady unless he pulls up even with us."

"Why?" she managed.

"Hoping this is a reconnaissance mission only." If he drew abreast of them, he could shoot into the car, or cause them to crash. Would he risk something so public?

She fought her racing pulse. Was Klee there to spy or slaughter?

"Hunch down," Tony said. "He doesn't know you're with us. Let's keep it that way."

The two miles seemed endless. The exit took them to a dimly lit road with a stop sign at the bottom of an ugly barren section of town with a few warehouses plopped along the road.

Tony shot her a look and he took her hand, caressing the fingers and sending sparks up her spine. His expression brimmed with worry and sincerity. "All I want out of this is for you and the kids to be safe. Your brothers too."

She read the apology in his eyes and squeezed back. "We're all going to make it. Everyone will be fine."

The phone beeped again. "We're in position," Levi said. "Roll to the stop sign and get down."

She swallowed hard. "Hey, Carter..." But she turned to find that he and Bee had finished their snacks and fallen asleep, hand in hand. Those little fingers clasped together awakened a rush of protectiveness, as strong as if she'd given birth to the children herself. The kids were not part of her precious Duke family, but at the moment, they felt every bit as important.

They've got to be okay, she prayed. *Please, Lord.*

She heard Tony unclick his seat belt as he pulled the car to a stop. With one hand on the door, he put the car into Park. Behind them, the Dodge's headlights blazed, blinding him. She heard Levi's truck roll from behind a warehouse, but she saw no lights. Peeking up just enough to see in the side view mirror, she caught the Dodge driver hit the brakes as he saw Levi's truck, and immediately reverse, crashing into Levi's front fender.

Willow stifled a cry as Tony leaped from the car, sprinting toward the Dodge, staying low. She peeked over the backseat to be sure Carter was still asleep, when Levi emerged from the truck, rifle aimed at the driver's window.

"Hands where I can see them," she heard

Levi shout. Austin approached the passenger side and Tony closed in on the other.

"Gun," Tony yelled as two shots exploded from the car. He hit the ground rolling. Levi returned fire, the shot pinging off the front fender. Had they been hit? Killed? Willow scrambled over the seat and covered Carter and Bee as best she could until she heard an engine revving. Risking a quick look she saw the Dodge jerk left and into a tight turn, careening around them and showering grit as Klee ran the stop sign before merging into the distant freeway and disappearing.

"I'll be right back," she said to Carter, who had awakened at the commotion. "Everything's okay." On shaky legs, she crept from the car. To her immense relief, all three men appeared to be unharmed. She breathed a silent prayer of gratitude.

Levi shouldered his rifle. "Anyone wounded?"

Tony brushed off his clothes. "We're all okay," he said, looking at Willow. "You and the kids?"

She nodded, hurrying to them. "Unbelievably, Bee slept through the whole thing. I think maybe Carter has fallen back asleep too. I don't think he saw anything."

Levi shook his head. "Let's get moving in case he doubles back."

"Agreed," Tony said, escorting Willow back to the car. He moved quickly, and she had to jog to keep up with his long strides. Back on the road, he checked the rearview every few minutes and she eyed her phone. No messages, nor sign of the Dodge. It didn't occur to her to ask until they rolled into Death Valley.

"If Klee tracks us to Furnace Falls, how will Ron make contact with you without getting caught?"

Tony's jaw clenched, and she knew there was no good answer.

Tony's migraine had subsided to a dull roar by the time they reached the airstrip outside of Furnace Falls. Exhaustion and throbbing pain had made the last few miles especially difficult. They finally drove the long graveled road and pulled into the empty covered hangar to find a small plane and another familiar vehicle already there. Uncle Gino had indeed beaten them, but Tony was so glad to get the children into a secure shelter, he didn't much care. They all needed sleep and safety, at least for a few hours.

The airstrip was a neatly tended paved strip. It cut through the gritty flat acreage which vanished into the burnished foothills beyond. Squatting on the property was a large rectangular two-story building, the lower floor serving as a habitable space and the upper floors reserved for storage and an office area, according to Austin. The outside could have used some paint, but it looked like a palace to him. Plus the visibility was fantastic.

Gino opened the door for them. "Took your sweet time."

"Hello to you too," Tony said, ushering Willow and Bee and Carter in ahead of him.

"Rustled up a couple of cots and put them in the biggest bedroom," Gino said. "Smaller bedroom ain't got room for an extra cot, but it has a full-sized rollaway and there's a shared bathroom for everyone at the end of the hall. I'll bunk on an air mattress in the office space upstairs. There's a toilet and a sink up there—all I need. Better lookout from that vantage point too." He knelt next to Carter and poked a gentle finger into his tummy. "You look tired, kiddo."

"He is," Willow said, her tone icy, before she switched her focus to Tony. "I'll change Bee and put them down for bed." Clearly, she was giving him time to fill Gino in. But should he?

Again the issue of whom to trust weighed like a bag of sand. He believed his uncle loved him, but Gino also maintained the only escape for Tony was for the kids to go to foster care.

The idea made Tony queasy. He was puzzling over what to reveal, when his uncle saved him from the decision by glancing at his phone. His thick brows cemented into an angry line. "Why am I getting a message from Severe that you were involved in an ambush?"

Tony stayed silent.

"You should have called me," Gino snapped.

"Don't trust anyone, remember? You told me that."

Gino folded his burly arms across his chest. "I'm family."

"So is Ron."

"Don't compare me to that clown. He's the reason you're in this mess. Why can't you understand that?"

"I do understand, but we're not talking about that now. I'm going to help Willow get the kids to bed and then I need sleep."

"If you're counting on that young lady and her kin to help get you out of this mess, they can't." Gino said. "I'm your only ally. Those Dukes will cut and run eventually, and you'll be alone with no one to help you."

Turning his back, Tony headed off to find the children, pondering his choices as he went.

One thing he knew without question. He trusted Willow. He didn't deserve her help, nor her family's, but he was grateful. The Dukes were involved because of Willow and he knew where their loyalty lay, but they were good people who would not betray him or the kids.

But with Klee tracking them relentlessly, would he be able to protect the children and keep Willow out of the line of fire?

He was too exhausted to hold on to the thought. He found them in the tiny bathroom at the end of a dark corridor. Willow's cheeks were puffed out as she demonstrated something to Carter, Bee balanced on her hip.

"We don't have a toothbrush," she said when she saw him. "But we found some mouthwash, which I diluted, so we're practicing the rinse and spit until we can buy some supplies."

She coached Carter through the process, and it was so endearing, all he could do was smile as he took Bee. Bee rested her cheek sleepily on his shoulder, Moo still gripped under her arm.

Willow and Carter exchanged a high five when the rinsing and spitting was complete. "There aren't enough sheets, but I found some clean blankets to use on the cots."

He helped her with Bee and then wrangled the blankets on the beds as best they could. She surveyed the stuffy room. "I can sleep in the rollaway with Bee if you want to bunk with Carter on the cots in here."

Practical, no matter what the circumstances. Willow didn't hesitate to adapt to whatever rolled her way. He realized he was staring at her again, the disheveled strawberry curls, the vivacious eyes that shifted from blue to gray depending on the light, the spunk in her that made him want to draw closer. Clearing his throat, he reached for Carter's shoulder. "All right. We'll sleep in the cots, just like Scout camp."

Carter's eyes were half-closed, and he flopped onto the cot with a sigh before Tony could kneel next to him to pray. He looked so small and pale lying there in the dingy room in yet another temporary home with none of his toys and no friends to play with save his baby sister.

Silently, Tony sank down and prayed with all his might that God would show him how to protect his temporary family. After the amen, he remained there, the dry floorboards creaking under his weight, listening to Carter's even breathing, feeling less like an uncle than a parent. He'd been so busy trying to provide, struggling against the yoke of being their whole world, that he had not quite noticed the moment he began to feel as if the children were his own. The uncle title had somehow settled into a deeper kind of love. It frightened him that he could have such unasked-for responsibility, but the Bible said it was possible to do anything that God wanted done. But being a substitute parent? Him? It was a tall order for a guy who couldn't even keep a houseplant alive.

"Thanks, God," he added, his voice only quavering a little, "for trusting me with them. And thank You for Willow and her family."

He kissed Carter gently on the forehead and managed to make it to his own cot, lying fully clothed and sinking immediately into sleep.

EIGHT

The next morning Willow awoke with a jolt, Bee curled up next to her belly. It took her a moment to remember where she was as her brain reported the details. Low ceiling with peeling paint, the aroma of a dusty mattress tickling her nose, hot sunlight pouring through a crack in ancient window blinds. The apartment at the airstrip. They'd somehow made it in spite of Gaudy's henchman. Bee and Carter and Tony were safe. She wasn't going to dwell on the fear of the previous couple of days. That chapter had ended. On to the next one.

After squirming out of the rollaway without waking Bee, she pulled on clothes and refreshed herself in the tiny bathroom. The building was warm already. June temperatures would generally climb into the hundreds, but they'd hovered in the mid-nineties the past week or two. Fortunate, since there was no air-conditioning.

Tiptoeing to the tiny kitchenette, she hoped there would be something there the kids could eat. Her own stomach was rumbling. Tony would be starved as well since he'd only eaten a bite of his sandwich the night before. Memories of Klee made her move faster. *Next chapter, remember?* The bad guys were on her turf now, in her town, with her people.

She entered the teeny space, surprised to find Mara there, frying eggs on the single burner.

"Good morning, Willow," Mara said, her long sweep of dark hair pulled into a neat ponytail. She squeezed her sister-in-law in a hug.

"Boy am I glad to see you. That smells wonderful."

Mara waved a spatula. "Hunger is the best seasoning. I brought supplies, and I figured I'd cook since I was here and it worked to sneak away from the ranch for an hour or two."

She raised a brow. "My brother let you come? He didn't think it was too dangerous?"

Mara gave her a steely glance. "Your brother doesn't 'let' me do things, Willow. We're married, but he isn't the boss of me and he knows it." She smiled. "And anyway, he's helping Austin with the plane in case you need to make a hasty departure. Our visit here is natural, since Levi comes all the time to help Austin.

Won't arouse suspicion if anyone in town is watching." She added salt to the sizzling pan. "I brought eggs, bread and cereal, milk, snacks for the kids. Pilar added baby supplies from Laney's stash since it would set all the town tongues wagging if she bought them."

Willow laughed. "Or if *you* did," she said slyly. "I know Levi would love to be a father and I'm ready to be Auntie Willow again anytime."

Mara wasn't rattled in the slightest. "Seems to me you're full up with kids at the moment. Anyway, Pilar said I should check on your state of mind because she knows what it's like to find out someone isn't who you thought they were." She paused. "You know, the big reveal that Tony isn't really Tony and everything that went along with that."

Willow grabbed a glass and filled it with water. "It was a shock, of course. But we're just friends and after this is over, I'll probably never see him again."

Mara paused. "And how does that make you feel?"

Willow gulped water a little too fast which set her coughing. "Tell Pilar I am fine, Dr. Mara. I don't need analysis. Tony's a friend, nothing more, and I'm providing a helping hand and staying here to make the protection easier for Marshal Diaz."

Mara was about to say something when Levi and Austin entered, Tony on their heels. A combination of uncertainty and the unavoidable observation that Tony was extremely attractive assaulted her. How did she feel? At that moment, friendship didn't seem to account for the sudden tremor in her nerves.

"Kids are both still sleeping," Tony said. He was clean-shaven now, so he must have found a razor somewhere. She pictured how he would look in his navy uniform before she caught herself. The navy service…was it the truth, or part of the web of lies he'd spun, albeit for good reasons?

"Are you okay?" Tony asked.

His probing glance made her jittery. "Fine." She distracted herself by accepting a plate of eggs from Mara and heading for the table, surprised when Tony pulled the chair out for her. She sank into it, knowing Mara's gaze was on her and hoping she was not blushing.

He was polite. So what? And handsome. Another trivial matter.

Levi and Austin sat at the table.

"Is your migraine gone?" she asked Tony after greeting her brothers.

"Not completely, but food will help," he said.

He gestured for Mara to sit with Willow since there were only three chairs and Levi and Willow were already seated.

Mara declined. "I already ate," she said. "You sit, Tony."

He did, and Willow caught the scent of soap that clung to his damp hair.

Levi finished his breakfast quickly and rinsed his plate. At this hour, he'd likely already been up since before dawn, scarfing down a slice of toast before he started his ranch chores. "Beckett said he hasn't noticed anyone but the normal flow of tourists in town, but he's keeping an eye out. He filled Jude in. Jude's been on the horn with Severe."

Willow forked in a mouthful of eggs. "Does Jude trust Severe?" If they knew that much, it would be a relief.

"Doesn't know him well enough personally, but his service record is exemplary."

Levi refilled his coffee cup from the pot. "That's not exactly a ringing endorsement from Jude."

"No, it isn't," Austin said. "So what's the game play? You all have a plan, right?"

Tony's cheeks went dusky. "Lay low and hope my brother arrives in the next week and a half like he said he would. If he does, I'm going to convince him to turn over what he has to Marshal Diaz and testify at the trial. They'll sequester him in a safe house."

"And you and the kids?"

"If Ron is cooperating, we'll still be under WITSEC protection." He looked at his laced fingers. "Another identity in a different place for us. No choice until Gaudy is put away and Ron can take them back."

Willow was struck by Tony's obvious pain. What would it be like to leave everything behind? She tried to imagine moving away from Furnace Falls, having no further contact with Levi, Austin, her parents, Beckett, his new baby. Everything.

"I wouldn't count on Ron showing up if I were you." Uncle Gino spoke from the doorway. "Morning," he said, strolling in. "I smelled eggs." Mara looked concerned until Tony introduced his uncle. Mara handled the situation with her typical gracious aplomb.

"Just consider me extra security," Gino told her, helping himself to eggs and leaning against the dingy wall while he ate. "Sheriff Severe called. He and Diaz are coming here in an hour or so." He flicked a glance at Tony. "Said they wanted a private meeting."

"Seems like the milk's already out of the jug," Austin said. "No point in keeping things secret from us, now, is there?" His words were friendly, but Willow recognized the tightness in his tone that indicated he was annoyed. Levi didn't answer, but he folded his arms, his body language declaring he intended on going nowhere anytime soon. Cowboy stubborn.

Mara looked from her husband to her brother-in-law. "Ooookay. I've got some supplies to unload for the kids before I head back to the ranch. Seth needs help with the tour bookings." She sighed. "He can't figure out the computer system to save his life. Doesn't help that he has short-term memory problems since the shooting." She arched a brow at the men. "You tough guys can finish the dishes while I unpack the boxes we hauled upstairs. I brought some toys that might keep the kids occupied."

Tony thanked her profusely. Willow felt giddy at the thought of clean clothes and proper toys for the children.

Gino washed and dried his dish. "Going to climb the control tower and have a look around. Don't get into any trouble while I'm gone."

Tony waited until they heard the front door bang. The conversation sputtered into silence that lasted too long.

"Just gonna put it out there because I'm that

kind of guy," Austin said. "Is your uncle an ally or not?"

Tony looked pained. "I wish I knew. He holds on to a heap of anger and resentment for trying to bail out my father. Dad's in jail for stealing from a company he was employed by, so you can see how well that worked out. Very humiliating for a cop to have a brother who can't stay on the straight and narrow. Gino loves me, no question, but he thinks Ron is cut from my father's cloth and he's determined to keep me from throwing my life away trying to save my brother."

"Because that's what he thinks he did," Willow said.

Tony nodded. "Took early retirement from the force to help care for us after my dad's first arrest. Family baggage."

"Which doesn't really answer my question," Austin said.

Tony thought a moment. "Gino would go against my wishes if he believed he could save me."

"Like putting the kids in foster care?" Willow wished she hadn't said it because Tony flinched as if she'd struck him.

"Yeah," he said. "But I have to admit I've wondered sometimes if he might be right." His voice hitched. "They deserve a stable home, and someone taking care of them who doesn't have to hide their identity and keep away from everyone else. What kind of life is that for a kid?"

Now it was her turn to squirm. If they'd been alone, she would have taken his hand for a friendly squeeze of encouragement. "They know you love them and they trust you," she reminded him. "Those are the two most important things right now."

Tony shot her a grateful look before he pushed his plate away. "What did you want to show me, Austin?"

Austin stood. "A way to get out quick if you need to." He paused. "Since it seems like Gino's actions are questionable, let's take a look at that tunnel before he comes back."

Tony turned to Willow. "I want you to see this too, just in case we get separated."

Willow swallowed. "I'll ask Mara to watch the kids for a few minutes."

Willow found Mara cross-legged on the floor with Carter. He gazed in fascination as she unloaded a half dozen wooden trains from a canvas sack. His obvious excitement made a lump in her throat.

"Wow," he said. "So many trains."

"They're my brother's," Mara explained

to Carter. "I had to promise him we'd return them, the big baby."

"Will your brother let me play with 'em?" Carter's voice was hushed with awe. "He's gonna share with me?"

"Yes, he will," Mara said. "For as long as you want."

"Really?" Carter began to line up the trains on the floor, oblivious to Mara and Willow.

"Bee is still sleeping," Mara said to Willow. "Plenty more eggs and toast for her when she wakes up."

Willow hugged Mara. "You are the best, you know that?"

"Just trying to keep up," she said. She agreed to watch the children, and Willow hurried to join Tony and her brothers. She couldn't imagine where there was a tunnel entrance, but they proceeded into a supply room past the bathroom at the end of the hallway. The cramped space was crowded with shelves and cleaning supplies, old buckets and a healthy collection of spider webs.

In the far corner was a trapdoor, revealed after they shifted some boxes around.

"Only reason I know about it is the guy who used to be the caretaker on this property showed it to me one time. Used to be an old mine shaft." Austin heaved up the stout wooden trapdoor, releasing a waft of cool air, perfumed with the smell of earth. Levi aimed a flashlight into the maw to reveal a steep wooden ladder. He climbed down without hesitation before calling up, "Twenty rungs down. Wood's solid."

Austin, Willow and Tony descended next. At the bottom of the ladder, Willow found herself on a dry earthen floor, surrounded by stone walls, roughly mortared into place. Another few yards farther, and the stone gave way to an earthen corridor, the low ceiling buttressed by stout timbers. A set of rail tracks wove away into the darkness.

"We'll go this way." Austin uncapped a container she hadn't seen him carrying and began to spray dots onto the floor that glowed in the light of Levi's flashlight as they walked on.

"Luminescent paint," Austin explained. "It'll be visible by flashlight. I'm going to mark the way to get out of here so you don't make a wrong turn if you have to use this as a getaway."

"What if we did make a wrong turn?" Willow asked.

"Don't," he said. "These tunnels go on for miles in all directions and much of it is on the brink of collapse. You'd be a fool to go exploring."

Levi raised a sardonic eyebrow. "Why does that remind me of a fool who did exactly that and sprained his ankle a few years back? On that particular occasion Jude and the fire department had to come extract him."

Austin huffed. "I have no idea who you're talking about."

"Right. We'll see what Jude says when he gets back." Levi continued up the tunnel. Tony moved close to Willow's elbow.

His whisper tickled her cheek. "Good to have an escape route."

"You think Klee will find us here?" she asked.

"No, we're safe. An extra precaution is all."

His words rang hollow. If they were discovered, would they have time to get the children and escape into the tunnels before they were caught? She ducked under a low beam. They passed a juncture where several other tunnels split off into the darkness. The air was heavy with the scent of moisture. "See what I mean?" Austin said, flicking his light at the shadowy passages. "Plenty of places to get lost or drop into an abyss or whatever." He kept spraying the glowing paint, three dots and then an arrow, a pattern he repeated as they went along.

Willow imagined the darkness was like

a giant snake, swallowing them up as they pressed forward. Chill bumps erupted on her skin and her slight case of claustrophobia wound her nerves tight.

You'll never have to use this escape, she told herself firmly. An extra precaution like Tony said.

And she hoped with all her might it was the truth.

Tony was beginning to wonder if they'd made a wrong turn in spite of Austin's guidance, when he halted and announced, "Here's the exit."

Tony did not detect any light penetrating the tunnel, but Austin had stopped at another ladder revealed by his flashlight beam. This one rose some fifty feet in the air, anchored into rock with iron brackets.

"Trapdoor at the top," Austin said. "Lets out about two miles from the hangar in a hilly area not far from the highway. You could hike easily back to the hangar or the main road if the heat didn't get you."

He imagined emerging into Death Valley's ferocious heat, toting Bee and Carter.

"I'll leave water and supplies at both entrance and exit points," Levi said, taking the words from Tony's mouth.

"For now we'd better head back for the meeting or Uncle Gino will come looking," Tony said.

Levi and Austin strode ahead, Willow and Tony trailing a few paces.

Following the glowing dots and arrows Austin had sprayed made the whole return trip an easy effort. If only he had such a scattering of markers to follow for the rest of his decisions. Was he doing the right thing waiting for Ron? Should he listen to Uncle Gino and wash his hands of his brother, put the kids in someone else's care?

Willow's hand slid into his, as if she could feel his emotional turmoil. He gripped it, with a flash of delight.

"You're doing the best you can," she said.

He huffed out a breath. "My best is not enough. I mean, they should have so much more. You know, Moo Moo, Bee's beloved toy? I got it as a freebie from the gas station mini-mart, some promotion or another. It's not even a proper kid toy."

"Bee doesn't care about proper. She loves Moo and she loves you. That proves you're giving them what they need."

Her touch was warm and strong, infusing him with unexpected comfort. "That means a lot that you think so, that you're even here with me after I lied to you."

She was quiet, but she did not relinquish his hand. "Did you... I mean, were you widowed, Tony?"

"No. Ron was. I've never been married."

It stabbed him, the lies he'd been forced to tell her.

"How about the navy thing? Was that a cover too?"

"Partially. I served in the navy, but I was an aircraft mechanic. My pilot's license is a private one. Did my four years and left to join the forest service as a pilot. It's what I always wanted to do. It's the best job I could ever have hoped for." The painful loss of it struck at him again.

She joggled his hand. "You'll get back to it someday."

He felt the same desperation that rose up when he let his guard down, the futile hope that he could somehow regain what he'd worked so hard for. Now that Klee was in the picture, and Ron running away from testifying, he had no right even to hope. "That dream looks far away at the moment."

She yanked at his arm now, teasing. "Put on your glasses then, Ortega. You can still see it on the horizon if you look in the right direction."

He was glad the darkness concealed his admiration. Was he actually temporary partners with this ebullient, fizzy woman with the rose-colored glasses? He had no business with such a person, even as a friend.

But friendship didn't quite encompass the sensation that crept across his heart. Impulsively, he brought her hand to his mouth and kissed her fingers. "Thank you."

He thought she might have sighed, but she pulled from his grasp. "Don't mention it. You needed a pep talk."

Not for the pep talk… He wanted to say, *for being who you are*…but she was already striding ahead.

A friend, he told himself firmly. And he was blessed to have one.

NINE

After their tunnel excursion, Mara left. Tony persuaded Carter to forego his trains long enough to eat a late breakfast while Levi and Austin went to sit in the living room, which was marginally cooler than the kitchen. Willow strapped Bee in the small booster seat that Mara had brought and cut her toast into slender sticks, which Bee waved as if she was conducting an orchestra.

"Hi, Bloney," she said, waving a toast stick at him.

Willow cocked her head at Tony. "Did she just call you Bloney?"

"She's trying to say baloney. It's her favorite lunch meat." He could only laugh. "That's me," he said, kissing her on the top of the head. "Good old Uncle Baloney."

Willow grinned. "I like it. Much better than Tony. Makes you sound more approachable."

"I'll take it," he said.

Diaz and Severe knocked on the door a few minutes later. Down the hall he could see Gino checking through the living room window before he allowed them to enter. Diaz looked impatient when she spotted Tony handing Carter a glass of milk, but she didn't interrupt. Good thing, since he wasn't about to let the kids do without. They'd already had plenty of that.

"I don't suppose they are coming with good news?" Willow whispered.

"Can't imagine how there's any good news to be had unless Gaudy has seen the error of his ways and turned himself in."

The meal concluded, they joined the others in the narrow living room and installed the kids on an area rug in a corner where there was a small TV, a sofa and a couple of cracked-leather recliners. A fan churned away overhead. Bee was quiet, happy to lie on her tummy with Moo and watch Carter play with his trains. Probably wasn't the best to let them sprawl on the floor. Who knew when it had been vacuumed last? What if they inhaled some dirt? Or maybe there were spiders? He'd read a newspaper article about a child who'd gotten a spider bite and…

He blinked as Willow touched his back. "They'll be fine."

"Right. Sure." Was his paranoia about the kids starting to be broadcast so clearly everyone could tell? In the cockpit, he was completely in control, unflinching. His sudden longing to be flying again nearly swamped him.

The grown-ups pulled together various unmatched wooden chairs and Tony and Willow shared a threadbare love seat. Another overhead fan struggled against the stuffiness.

Gino shrugged at Diaz. "Told Tony it was supposed to be a private meeting."

Levi said nothing. Austin smiled. "Don't mind us. We're here for sis. Consider us her civilian security team."

"Civilian interference gets people killed," Diaz said.

"We're not your average civilians." There was something dangerous in Levi's abrupt remark. Diaz stared at him for a moment before she turned to Tony.

"Now that I've finally got details about your little dustup on the freeway last night, I'm sure Gaudy's obviously gotten a report from Klee. Did he see Willow?"

"No, and the clerk in the gas station asked only about me and the kids," Tony said. "I don't think Klee knows who Willow is yet."

She exhaled. "Good. Then the airport safe house may work for a while, since he knows a woman is helping you but he doesn't know who. Buys us the time we need. Have you heard from your brother?"

"No."

Diaz watched him for a few seconds, probably gauging his truthfulness, or hoping he would start talking to alleviate the silence. He took a page from Levi's book and stayed quiet.

"We got some intel that Ron did cross the border into Canada yesterday morning, but we lost him there. That part of his story checks out."

"Ron loves Canada. Used to travel there all the time with his late wife. That's where she was born." Bee coughed, and Tony jerked a look at her. The little girl had a bad habit of putting things into her mouth. She'd even stuffed a pebble up her nose at one point. It was only a cough though, not a breathing obstruction. He turned his attention back to Diaz.

"So you believe whatever he's retrieving could really be valid proof against Gaudy?" he said.

"Possibly. We have a tech guy who managed to back door into Gaudy's operation for only a few moments before he was detected and shut down. He thinks Ron might have been able to download files with dark web client information too, since he likely had access for a longer period."

"If anyone could, it's my brother. The internet has always been his playground. He told me before Christmas that he'd taken a job as an accountant for this rich guy on his property in Malibu."

"Gaudy," Severe confirmed.

"Ron didn't tell me all the details, but he said he'd gotten to know the guy's wife, Eugenia. Ron's wife died when Bee was six months old, so I figured he was lonely, and he'd found someone to talk to. He complained that Gaudy was arrogant and thought he was smarter than everyone including Eugenia and Ron. Ron said he was going to prove to the rich guy that it wasn't true." Tony sighed. "I was only half listening, to be honest. My job with the forest service was going great and Ron always had some kind of scheme in the works. Always trying to prove something. Once he said the kids were okay, I tuned him out until the marshals showed up with the kids and explained that Gaudy was being charged and Ron was a key witness."

Diaz drummed her fingers on the legs of her uniform pants.

"What about the judge? Was she intimidated

into the postponement? Maybe as a way to give Gaudy time to locate Ron?" Willow asked.

Diaz looked surprised. "Where did you get that idea?"

Willow stayed quiet and waited for an answer.

Diaz shook her head. "I can't confirm that."

Willow and Tony exchanged a look. Not exactly an answer.

"If this judge bails, we'll get another," Diaz said. "Our job is to ensure Ron is alive to testify. And if we had more concrete proof, this thumb drive Ron's claiming for instance, we'd have a much better chance at convicting Gaudy."

Tony shoved his fingers through his hair. "But like I explained, he's not intending to deliver what he has to you. He's figuring on a blackmail payout."

"Then he's a fool," Diaz said.

"No argument there," Gino said.

Diaz shook her head. "Gaudy posted bail within an hour of his arrest and he never goes anywhere unprotected. I can't even begin to tell you how much damage he's caused. We're talking big stakes here. There are illegal guns on the street because of Gaudy, drug deliveries, even murder for hire scenarios all worked out via his dark web connections."

"I know the stakes are high," Tony snapped. "You don't have to remind me."

"I think I do, in case your sense of brotherhood gets in the way. There's only one plan that gets you your life back. When he contacts you, convince him to give us what he has, and come back to testify," Diaz said, staring at Tony.

"What makes you think I can?"

She pointed to the children. "You have very two compelling reasons."

Tony's teeth ground together. "They're not bargaining chips."

"Like it or not, they are," Severe said, but Tony caught a regretful tone in the sheriff's voice.

"He might not even come back here," Willow said. "Maybe he'll ask Tony to meet him with the children someplace else, after he's already worked out his blackmail scheme."

"Then we'll be there because Tony will tell us the location," Gino said. "Right?"

Tony felt suddenly smothered. He stood abruptly. "You're asking me to betray my brother."

"In order to save his kids." Diaz stood too. Severe continued to watch from his seat. "Klee almost got you, Tony, and he would have taken Carter. You know that's the truth."

He recalled Gaudy's high nasal voice. *You're done, Tony. All you can influence is time.*

But that did not horrify him as much as Klee's heinous pronouncement.

The boy... I'll keep him... I'll be his dad. He's gonna call me Pops, like I called my dad.

A trickle of cold sweat chilled his back. He breathed the panic away in time to hear Diaz ask him, "I'd like permission to put a bug on your phone."

"Why?" Dumb question.

"To track any texts or messages that come in from Ron," she said coolly.

Should he? Shouldn't he? "I'll think about it."

Diaz glowered, but Severe lumbered to his feet. "Fair enough. I'd suggest you lay low while you're waiting to hear from Ron. Nobody unusual in town, but you never know. If you do venture out, remember to make it fast and no chitchatting around town." He jutted a chin at the children. "There's a nice ice-cream parlor in town across from the police station. No safer place if you need a fast outing. Order the cones to go."

"An outing can wait," Diaz said.

Severe raised a thick eyebrow at her. "I can tell you haven't spent a ton of time around the preschool set." He waved at Bee, who wriggled her foot in a return greeting, sending her pink shoe flying.

"I have to go into town to take care of some details for my business," Willow said.

"No," Diaz said.

"It's my livelihood. I have to go."

Diaz relented. "Fine, but remember Klee is good at finding things out. If he comes to town, it won't take him long to target you."

Tony was about to say it didn't sound "fine" to him to have Willow wandering the town unprotected, but he saw from the calculating look on her brothers' faces that they intended to keep tabs on her.

"Keep us in the loop, huh?" Severe said as they left and Gino locked the door behind them.

Was he referring to contact with Ron or any plans to take the kids into town? Tony wasn't sure.

Par for the course, since he wasn't sure about one single thing anymore.

Willow sat with the kids until a beep from her phone calendar reminded her that she had a project to finish and send, some panoramic photos she'd taken from Zabriskie Point. Since

Brad had stolen the digital prints from a whole years' worth of photos, she was anxious to build up another stockpile of work she could both sell to clients and license for internet use. She'd finished editing them to perfection, so all that remained was to email them to her client.

It didn't feel like the right time to go into town, with Klee on the prowl, but most of her bread and butter came from the photography tours she led and those had all but dried up as the summer approached. No way she could turn her back on her hard-won business until the Tony situation was handled. Since the files were on her computer at her miniscule office space in town, she was going to have to make a trip, whether she wanted to or not. She was about to tell Tony she was leaving, when his phone buzzed.

The expression on his face when he checked the screen kicked up her pulse. "What? What is it?"

"A text from Ron." He held it up so they could both see. His muscled shoulder pressed against hers.

I got what I needed. Gonna get the kids soon. Taking them to Mexico after I hit up Gaudy. He's gonna pay. Where are you?

Tony texted back quickly. Klee is after us. Can't tell you right now. You gotta go to the marshals.

No can do. I will arrange a meeting spot for you to bring kids to me. Then I'm gonna leave the country. Sorry, bro. Gotta do this.

With a groan, Tony tried dialing his brother, but Ron didn't answer.

"Leave the country with the kids?" Tony said as he pocketed the phone. "How's he going to do that when Klee has their passports?"

"You can do it with birth certificates if you're a parent, I think," Willow said. "Even if he can't, working near Gaudy he probably knows of a few people who can forge documents."

He blew out a long, slow breath. "I'll call Diaz and tell her what he's planning. I don't see that I have much choice."

She touched his arm. "You're doing the best you can. Ron will have to understand that."

"He and I don't think on the same frequency. We never have."

"Are you worried you won't be able to convince him to talk to Diaz?"

Tony groaned. "Probably easier to convince a lion to become a vegetarian."

Willow helped Tony get Bee down for her after-lunch nap before she grabbed her purse. "Be back in an hour." She rolled her eyes. "And yes, rest assured that one of my brothers is going to be lurking around somewhere stalking me."

He stopped her as she approached the front door. "I um…" A rising color stained his face. "I know you're fully capable of handling anything, but please be careful. If Klee hurt you, I would never forgive myself."

All the blood seemed to rush to her head, leaving her dizzy. "Everything's okay. No worries."

He sighed. "No, it's not. Willow, this is awful. I mean…you're trapped on an old airstrip and you can't even walk around your own hometown. It's all so…fake. We're not even dating and…" He trailed off.

The word *fake* stabbed at her. Why, she did not know. Of course it was all fake, and Tony was a friend, nothing more, but an ache started up in her chest that made it hard to breathe. She'd imagined pursuing a relationship with Brad, only to find out he wasn't even honest, let alone loving. Tony, she knew deep in her soul, was honest. But this wasn't love. It was purely survival.

"It's okay," she said. "If my being here is

helping you and the kids, I'm happy to do it. Safer for me too, right?"

His eyes lingered on hers. "You deserve way more than that." And then he leaned in. Her heart whammed a million miles an hour, as he pressed a kiss lightly on her lips.

He moved away while the sparks were still dancing. "I won't be long," she managed.

A kiss? A friendly peck to him, of course, but her whole being lit up like a sparkler on July Fourth. *Stop*, she scolded internally. *He's a friend, a good friend who wants the best for you just like you do for him.* Nonetheless, her legs were shaky as she hurried to her Jeep and raced off the airstrip.

TEN

She managed her errand quickly. Each moment she lingered in her office made her antsy to return to the airstrip. Allowing one more minute, she grabbed the messages off her answering machine and let herself out, locking the door behind her.

"Hey there," she heard. Spinning around she found her friend Vanna, a nurse in the doctor's office, licking an ice-cream cone as she strolled the sidewalk. A big straw hat covered her head. "Hi, Willow. I'm on my lunch break so I thought I'd come see if I could catch you at work. I heard some stuff about you, girl." Vanna swept Willow with a searching look. "Where have you been? I stopped by your apartment to see if you wanted to go to the movies, but the manager said you hadn't been home for a while." Her eyes glittered. "Someone told me they saw you driving with a handsome man. What's his name? I heard he has kids. How many? Spill it, before I explode."

Heat rose in her belly and crawled up her throat. "I…um…"

"Hey, sis," Austin said, rolling his truck up to the curb and calling through the open window. "Hop in. Don't wanna be late, right?"

Relief welled up in Willow. "Right. Sorry I can't talk right now, Vanna. Good to see you."

She climbed in and they drove off, leaving Vanna looking curiously after them.

She blew out a breath. "Thank you, Austin."

"Anytime. Looked like you needed a save."

"I didn't think it would be so hard to keep everyone fooled."

"Never were much of a liar. Couldn't even keep a secret under pain of sibling retaliation. You told everyone about our top-secret lair when we were kids. I don't think Levi has ever gotten over it."

She laughed. "Guilty."

He chuckled. "We'll give Vanna a few minutes and I'll drop you back at your Jeep when the coast is clear. Good thing we had your busted windows repaired. The bullet holes would be hard to explain."

"What would I do without you?"

He pretended to mull it over. "You'd have

to settle for Levi, and he's in no way as cool a brother as I am."

"I won't tell him you said that." Austin was looking at her. "Tony is pretty concerned when you're out of his sight."

She knew her face had gone fiery. "Uh, yeah. He, uh, just feels responsible."

He thrummed the steering wheel. "He is. The way you got ensnared in this is crummy."

"I…"

"But Tony's a good guy, though Levi would swallow his tongue before he admitted it."

She blinked. "How can you say that? You don't even know Tony."

"You can judge a guy by how he treats his children, or the children around him anyway, and Pilar wouldn't agree, but I can recognize a brewing romance when I see one."

"Austin," she said firmly. "Tony and I are not like that. We're friends."

He shrugged. "Okay, whatever." He raised a mischievous eyebrow. "But I mean he's a dashing pilot, and those types are irresistible so…"

She poked him in the shoulder.

"Watch it, sis. I got damaged parts, remember?" He grinned.

Austin pulled to the corner when his phone rang. "Hey, Levi. Got Willow here. I rescued her from a nosey friend." He put it on speaker.

"Beckett said there was a stranger trying to get a room at the Hotsprings," Levi said. "Struck Beckett as odd 'cuz the guy wanted to pay in cash and book day to day. Guy left as soon as Beckett said he didn't have any vacant rooms, and so far he's nowhere in town. Beckett couldn't get his photo, but he called Diaz to come check out the footage from the parking lot camera. No help. He had a cap pulled over his face and he stayed out of camera reach for the most part."

Willow chewed her lip. "Can Beckett describe him?"

"Short, stocky, dark hair."

"Could describe a ton of people," Austin said.

Her mouth went dry. "Or just one really dangerous one. Klee."

"I showed Beck a photo, but he can't make a positive ID with the glasses and cap."

Austin's good humor was gone. "Okay, Levi. Thanks for the info. Escorting her back to the safe house now." He disconnected.

Willow didn't wait for him to dive in. "I know, I know. I'll go back to the airstrip and try to stay there as much as I can without tanking my business."

"That's music to my ears, and it will prevent Levi from developing an ulcer. You know those quiet types. Killer on the health." His playfulness did not fully mask his concern.

They continued through the town and she waved to a friend crossing the road on foot. Had everyone heard she'd vacated her apartment? She did a double take as she saw a familiar person walking out of the local hardware store. Uncle Gino. Checking things out, as he claimed to be doing? He stopped and stared in the direction of her store and lingered there in the shade of an awning. Then he fished out his phone and took a couple of pictures. He had to be aiming at her office, and the Duke's Photography sign. After another few moments, he got into his car and drove away.

"He's showing a lot of interest in your shop," Austin said, frowning.

"Considering security?"

"Possibly."

His tone was unconvinced, and she felt the same way. She did not like Uncle Gino, in spite of his professed love for Tony. The easy way he suggested consigning the children to foster care and betraying Ron stuck in her craw. And yet he was now installed at the airstrip, watching every move Tony made.

Wouldn't be hard for him to feed information to the police.

Or Gaudy.

Safely back at her vehicle, she thanked Austin and climbed into her Jeep, her nerves screaming at her to return to Tony and the kids.

Willow realized something was wrong before she got out of the cot on Sunday morning. It hadn't been a satisfying sleep, worries rattling around in her head about what might happen as they waited for Ron to contact them. Since Beckett had made a possible Klee sighting, the tension had escalated. Now as she struggled into consciousness, she felt Bee's warm body next to hers, a little too warm. Willow flicked on her phone light to examine the child.

Bee's cheeks were red and her forehead was hot, but the most frightening detail was that her breathing was labored and gurgly. Willow immediately threw on clothes and knocked on Tony's door. He opened it quickly, fully dressed, but the shadow on his chin indicated he had not yet shaved. Carter was asleep on the cot.

"I think Bee's sick," she explained.

His face blanched. "Do you have a good doctor in town?"

"Only one, Dr. Howley. I called him when we got to town to schedule a physical, but it's not until next week. Today is Sunday, no office hours. I'll call his service and they can refer us." She chewed her lip. "He's got a partner doc who works at the clinic in Copper Ridge, but it's twenty minutes from here. I'm sure that's where they'll send us."

He looked at his watch. "It's seven thirty. When do you think they open?"

"Eight. I had to give Laney a lift over there last week to pick up a humidifier Dr. Howley ordered from the clinic pharmacy."

"Okay. I'll get Carter up and we'll take them both."

She knew why. Because he didn't trust Gino with Carter. Neither did she. "Let me ask my family to come stay with Carter, instead."

He hesitated.

"It would be less risk and both my brothers know how to handle themselves."

"I know they do. Okay. Give them a call." He hesitated. "I'll phone Diaz too, to be on the safe side. At least, I think that's the smart thing to do."

His frown said he wasn't sure, but how could they travel without alerting law enforcement if Klee really was in the area? Again, she wished her cousin Jude would hurry back from his training.

They quickly made their phone calls. Fifteen minutes later, Willow let Austin and Pilar in.

"Levi's on a tour, so you get the dynamic duo here." Austin pulled Pilar into his good shoulder and kissed her temple. "She's the best-looking wingman in the history of wingmen."

Pilar smiled. "I'm real good at keeping a lookout and dialing 9-1-1."

Austin lowered his voice to a whisper. "And Seth's parked in the bushes near the airstrip entrance so he can alert us in time to get Carter into the tunnel and out of here. He was thrilled to be asked."

Relieved, Willow thanked them again, hurried to Bee's room and roused the sleepy girl enough to get her into a clean diaper and the clothes Mara had provided. Bee looked adorable in the pink-ruffled jumper, but she was peevish.

Tony was helping Carter into a T-shirt unaware of her presence as she hurried to find him.

"We're gonna take sissy to the doctor and get her some medicine. Austin and Uncle Gino will stay with you, okay?" Tony said to Carter.

Abruptly, Carter's face puckered, and he threw his arms around Tony, sniffling. Willow's heart ached. He'd been through so much terror in the past few days, seeing his father run away again, the abduction—it was no wonder he was terrified to hear that Tony was leaving, even only temporarily.

"Hey, buddy. It's going to be okay." Tony held him close. "I'll come back. I will take care of you and your sister. I promise." Carter relinquished his hold, and Tony rubbed his hair. "Remember how we pray when we're scared, right?"

Carter nodded. "Uh-huh."

Tony folded his big palms around Carter's small fingers. "Lord, we trust You and we love You in the good times and the bad. Amen."

Willow added her own silent "amen."

When they were finished, Tony turned and spotted Willow.

"I didn't know you were there. Carter's ready to play in the living room."

She blinked back a wash of tears at what she'd seen. Tony's sweet comfort to Carter cleaved sparks in her soul. "Sure," she managed, following them down the hallway. There was so much she didn't know about Tony, so many deceptions he'd been forced to embrace, but what she'd seen in that tender moment was genuine, sacrificial love. The small vignette kicked off a trail inside her and she knew she'd done the right thing committing to helping Tony.

You're standing up for a friend, she told herself, *and there's nothing more to it. Keep it straight.* They hustled through the last-minute preparations.

Pilar and Carter sat on the area rug and began to line up the trains while Austin pulled all the curtains closed and checked the doors.

Uncle Gino sauntered down the stairs. "I heard from Severe. He's on his way over."

So Severe was feeding information to Gino? Or was it Diaz?

She saw the slight tightening of Tony's mouth.

"I'll follow you," Gino said. "You've got enough protection here with Severe and your civilian brigade."

"Following us will only draw more attention," Willow said.

He laughed. "Cop, remember? I know how to tail someone."

Tony hesitated, which made Gino frown. "I'm here to protect you." He went to the window and flipped the curtain back. "Severe will do slow circles until we return. He'll be here in five. I'll climb the tower for a quick look and give you a three-minute head start. If we need to abort, I'll text you."

She filled a bag with fishy crackers and a sippy cup of cold water and went with Tony to the car. She strapped Bee in, the motion setting off a coughing jag from the little girl.

Tony gripped the wheel as Willow buckled herself into the passenger seat. They headed off the airstrip and onto the main road and then to the highway that took them to Copper Ridge. The town was larger than Furnace Falls. Even so, the clinic was a modest-sized, one-story stucco building that housed an urgent care department and a few small offices. Next to it was a reasonably sized pharmacy. Willow didn't see any signs that Uncle Gino or anyone else was following as she and Tony whisked Bee into the clinic.

Tony filled out the paperwork. They went with Bee into a room where a rotund Dr. Gordon did an exam, dazzling Bee with a rubber glove he blew up into a balloon. "She'll need a little medical support," he said. "Here's a prescription for you to fill at the pharmacy next door and I'll arrange through your local doc for a visiting nurse to administer a home breathing treatment," he said, bobbing the balloon at Bee.

Tony and Willow exchange a look. A visitor?

The doctor reassured them. "Her name is Inez Parker, and she's a gem. I'll email you the appointment time." He clacked away on his keyboard until the screen went dark. Frowning, he fiddled with the power cord connection. After a moment, the machine came back to life. He finished his notes. "You can expect Inez tomorrow for the next treatment."

Tony sighed. "Thank you very much, Doctor."

"You're welcome. Don't look so worried, son. This parenting thing is hard, but you two make a good team."

A good team... Willow scooped up Bee as Tony gathered the diaper bag. They exited the building and into the sauna-like temperatures. His phone buzzed and he checked the text.

"It's Uncle Gino." Tony's eyes went wide. "He thinks he spotted Klee."

Tony clicked the unlock button for the car and was reaching for the handle when the sound of a gunned engine deafened her.

Willow clutched Bee as a sedan beelined for them across the empty parking lot.

"Get in," Tony yelled, yanking open the passenger door and tumbling them in. The rubber glove balloon the doctor had given Bee floated away.

Willow had barely closed the door and hit the lock, Bee on her lap, when Tony leaped behind the steering wheel and cranked on the motor. They were too slow, caught off guard, and the sedan pulled in behind them, blocking them in.

Willow saw out the side mirror as Klee rushed to the passenger door, yanking on it.

Tony shouted as Klee raised the butt of his gun to the glass and rammed it, sending cubes of safety glass raining down on Willow and Bee. She screamed and held on as Klee grabbed her arm and yanked them both toward him. Bee cried out, and Willow did the only thing she could think of, biting the sinewed wrist in front of her face as Tony flung open his door and ran to the passenger side.

There was a howl as Klee recoiled, right into Tony's raised fist. He stumbled back, and Tony was able to aim a nasty kick at his kneecap that would likely have crippled him if he hadn't dodged to the side.

Raising the gun, he faced off with Tony.

"Mr. Gaudy wants to use the kids to get Ron, but he don't mind if you die in the process," Klee panted.

"No," Willow shouted, heaving Bee's sippy cup at Klee, who easily batted it away, but Tony had used the moment to lunge toward the man, his head connecting with Klee's stomach. Klee gasped, staggered, but kept his footing.

Willow's blood turned to ice. What could she do that wouldn't further endanger Bee?

Attract attention. Diaz, Uncle Gino, anyone. Scooting quickly she laid her elbow on the horn and kept it there.

The noise echoed through the parking lot. Someone had to notice.

"Knock it off," Klee snarled.

But Willow kept the horn blast going, trying to angle her body around Bee in a futile attempt to protect her if Klee decided to shoot.

There was the pounding of booted feet.

"US Marshal," Diaz shouted as she appeared around a parked car, gun raised in a double-handed grip.

Klee shoved Tony, who stumbled and fell backward, crashing into Diaz. Willow clutched Bee. Diaz and Tony both scrambled to their feet.

"Get in your vehicle and drive out of here," Diaz ordered before she holstered her weapon and sprinted through the parked cars in the direction Klee had taken. Willow moved over to the passenger seat, trying to comfort Bee. They had to get away.

Uncle Gino appeared in a squeal of tires as Tony backed out of the space. "Keep going," Gino shouted and wheeled the car around to pursue Diaz. Tony's eyes danced between the rearview mirror and the front windshield. Their panted breaths were overshadowed by

Bee's wailing. When they were a good mile from the clinic, he pulled to a quiet corner, engine running and took Bee from Willow's shaking grasp.

Bee wailed, "Bayoon," at the top of her lungs.

"It's okay, Bee Bee," he said, kissing her. "We'll get you another balloon."

Willow handed over Moo, which placated the child enough that he could buckle her in the car seat after Willow carefully checked it for bits of glass. They resumed their positions and drove back out of town toward the airstrip.

The shock of what had transpired left her wobbly. Klee had come so close.

He reached for her hand, his long fingers comforting, his touch warm on her clammy skin. "You okay?"

"Yes. You?"

He shrugged. "Banged up a smidge, but A-okay." He glanced again at Bee in the backseat. "As long as you and Bee aren't hurt, I'm peachy." He quirked his mouth, "Nice use of the teeth." The comment made her smile, but she knew they were both still reeling from the close call.

"Thanks," she said. "Good thing I brush and floss."

"Klee has definitely seen your face now," Tony said, a crease between his brows. "Maybe you should leave the airstrip. Go hide out in your apartment."

"He can get me there easier than the airstrip," she pointed out. "Like Diaz said."

They didn't speak much for another few miles and she was glad Tony left his hand on her arm.

"Gino's warning came a little late," he said.

"Do you think he's in on it?"

"I don't know. How did Klee know we were headed for the clinic? Who knew besides the two of us? Diaz and Severe?"

"And my brothers."

"Uncle Gino," he said darkly.

"But your uncle wants you safe."

"Maybe. Or maybe he figured letting Gaudy have what he wants would get him off my back."

"I don't like your uncle, Tony, but I have to believe he would not give Bee up to Klee to get his own way."

"I don't know what to believe," Tony said. His touch slid away as he gripped the wheel. "Or whom."

She looked at the deep lines around his mouth. "You know you can trust me though, Tony. Don't you?"

"Yes." He let out a breath. "You're the only

one I really do trust. I know you'll do your best for the kids until this is all over."

All over.

She blinked. Do what's best for the kids. Then their connection would be unnecessary.

And Tony will vanish from your life like the stars from the morning sky.

She vowed to remember that as they hurried back to the airstrip.

ELEVEN

Tony was nearly finished relating the story to Austin and Pilar when Diaz and Uncle Gino returned. Severe joined them too.

Tony had put a cartoon video in the old DVD player, and Carter and Bee were watching, mesmerized.

"What a train wreck," Gino said.

"Lower your voice," Tony commanded. "I don't want the kids to hear."

"I lost him," Diaz said with a scowl. "I got some intel from the car he abandoned. He used a fake ID for the rental, but it was Klee, no doubt."

Austin's brows drew together. "Pretty risky to attempt a snatching in a public parking lot during daylight hours,"

"Gaudy is not what you'd call a patient man," Diaz said. "Klee wasn't making progress fast enough would be my guess, and he's getting pressure to deliver as the trial date draws closer."

Tony sat rigid on his chair. "How did Klee know we would be going to the clinic at that time?"

Gino's hands went to his hips. "Good question. We gotta leak, Diaz?"

She met his hard stare with one of her own. "Not from this end."

"And not from mine either," he said.

"Don't look at us." Austin patted Pilar's knee. "We're just here to play with trains."

Willow noticed a message on her cell phone. She listened and then huffed out a breath. "Better hear this." She thumbed it to replay over the speaker.

"Hi, Willow, it's Vanna." Her voice was lacking its usual ebullience. "This may be nothing, but I thought it was weird. Someone called here just before closing time yesterday claiming they were new to town and looking for a doctor. Said their friend Tony recommended our place and asked if they'd gotten the right business and was Tony Ortega really a client. I told them I couldn't say, for confidentiality reasons. I thought it was weird, you know? Anyway, I would have checked where the number originated from, but early this morning our phone systems went down and everything was erased. What a pain that was. Anyway, I just wanted to tell you about that call. She might have been purely innocent, but it rubbed me the wrong way."

"She?" Tony and Willow said at the same time.

"She," Diaz said. "In a way, we shouldn't be surprised. Gaudy commands plenty of people, or he might have gotten his wife, Eugenia, to make the call. No doubt he's punishing her for betraying him with Ron."

Willow shuddered. "Poor woman, being married to that man."

Diaz shrugged. "Guy she dated before Gaudy was a drug smuggler, so she knows how to pick 'em."

"So she's sniffing out information, but that doesn't quite explain how they knew we were going to the clinic," Tony continued.

"Yes, it does," Willow said miserably. "Dr. Howley is the only pediatrician in town. I called and left a voice mail for Dr. Howley with his answering service asking for that physical appointment since Mrs. Finley said to have Bee looked at. I gave her name as Bee Ortega. When Vanna said their phone systems went down…"

Tony swallowed. "It was actually Gaudy's people tampering with them."

"And listening to the message about Bee," Gino finished. "When you called again this morning, they were privy to the message directing you to the clinic."

Tony tried not to give in to the fear clawing at his stomach.

Diaz sighed. "I told you he can get anything he wants via his dark web. Soon as there was confirmation Bee was a patient at the clinic, Gaudy got a hacker to monitor their messages in the hopes you'd call back. When you did, Klee was notified and dispatched to intercept."

Tony's teeth ground together.

"Call your brother," Diaz demanded. "Immediately. Tell him you need to meet. It's urgent."

"I..." But Tony looked at Willow, remembered Klee trying to pull her and Bee from the car. If he'd succeeded... A lump formed in his throat. Wordlessly, he took out his cell phone and dialed.

No answer.

When it kicked to voice mail, he explained what had happened.

"I know you love your kids, Ron. You've got to bring the marshals what they need to put Gaudy away. Now."

Or you might lose your kids altogether.

And he might lose Willow.

Lose her? That awakened a surge of confusion. She wasn't his to lose. Was she?

His cell rang, and he stared dumbly at it.

"Everybody quiet," Diaz said, signaling him to put it on speaker.

"He's gonna pay," Ron almost yelled into the phone. "Gaudy is gonna pay for what he's done. He could have killed you."

"Listen," Tony thundered. Ron sputtered to a stop. The kids looked at Tony so he forced a smile and controlled his volume, positioning his back to them. "Gaudy is closing in, and you can make him pay by sending him to jail. Hand over your proof and testify against him. It's the only way, Ron."

"You don't get it. He'll slither out of jail time. I want him to sweat, to realize that I hold the cards, not him. I'm calling him today, Tony. I'm telling him that he's going to leave off terrorizing you and give me enough money to bankroll a life for me and the kids. He'll do it and he'll be sorry he ever tangled with me."

"No, he won't," Tony said, through gritted teeth. "He'll murder us all."

"I'll take care of it, I promise. Have the kids ready, okay? As soon as I contact Gaudy and he transfers the money to my account, I'm on a plane to Mexico with the kids. Then I'll mail the proof back to the States when I'm settled. Like I said, he'll weasel out of any jail time, but it will disrupt his operation and that's enough for me."

"Ron…" Tony started.

"I'll meet you and the kids tomorrow in Rhyolite. It's an old, abandoned town, easy visibility. Hardly any tourists this time of year. Can you find it?"

Tony looked at Willow, who nodded.

"Yeah, but…"

"Ten a.m. Tomorrow. This is gonna work out, Tony. You'll see."

The line went dead. Frustration nearly choked off Tony's oxygen supply.

"Well, at least we have a meet time and location," Diaz said. "If Ron lives long enough."

Uncle Gino huffed out a breath. "With Gaudy and his people everywhere? I give him zero chance."

Tony looked at Diaz. "What can I do? How can I help make this turn out okay?"

Diaz extended a hand. "Just to be certain, let me put a bug on your phone. If you'd allowed it before, we could have had a direct bead on him right now."

And Ron might be saved from making a fatal mistake.

"Maybe we can trace the cell signal to get a

general area, but he'll probably be on the move so that won't help. I'll place the bug, you'll message him again with some follow-up questions. We'll pick him up."

Nausea nearly choked Tony. In order to save Ron, he was going to have to betray him. There was no other way. He stared at his phone, frozen with the weight of what he was about to do. Shooting a look at the children paralyzed him completely. *Lord, am I doing the right thing?*

Willow put her hand on the small of his back. She didn't speak, but he felt her encouragement, her belief in him, and it infused him with just enough energy to unlock his muscles. He gave Diaz the phone.

"Good choice," she said. "Give me a couple of hours."

What would a couple of hours bring?

His brother's death?

Or Gaudy's one-way trip to prison?

Tony paced the kitchen floor, sock footed to keep from awakening anyone. He'd abandoned all attempts at sleep and it was still not even 2:00 a.m. He'd been up past midnight with Diaz, Severe and Uncle Gino working out the plans for the meet with Ron. He'd messaged his brother with a follow-up question as Diaz directed, but Ron had not replied so they had no choice but to go forward with the meeting and hope Ron showed.

Since there was no way he would risk Willow or the children, they would stay put at the airstrip. At least he'd know if things went bad, they wouldn't be caught in the cross fire.

The swinging door squeaked and Willow padded in, barefoot, in sweats and an oversize T-shirt that dwarfed her small form. Her hair was tousled, freckles pronounced against her pale skin.

She quirked a coppery brow at him. "No sleep for you either?"

"No," he said. "Too hot." *And too many worries.*

"Snack?"

"Sure."

He watched in amusement as she built two peanut butter and banana sandwiches and poured glasses of milk into which she swirled some chocolate syrup Mara had provided.

She took in his surprise. "What? Don't like PB and banana? It worked for Elvis."

He laughed. "Well, if it's good enough for the King of Rock and Roll..." He settled at the table with her, took a bite, and washed it down with the chocolate milk. "Man, I forgot how good chocolate milk is."

She sighed. "Yep, and the sandwich is better

with chunky peanut butter, but beggars can't be choosers and all that." She wiped her mouth on a paper napkin. "Worried about Ron?"

"Very. That's nothing new, except for the three years he was married to Kathy. I don't know how, but she gave him focus, inspired him to make responsible life decisions. She tempered his wild side." He sighed. "She had this light that kind of lit up everyone around her." He paused. "Like you."

Willow ducked her head and he realized he'd said too much. He hurried on. "When she died, it ruined him and he lost his way. Working for Gaudy brought in the money and the affair he had with Eugenia was another catastrophic step in a series of bad choices. He's wrecked everything."

She cocked her head. "But you love him anyway."

"I do. Love is not dependent on behavior." He chuckled. "God reminds me of that constantly, most recently when Bee flushed an entire roll of toilet paper and a stack of Dixie Cups down the toilet. Love withstands all things, but toilet plumbing does not. Anyway, Ron had a great relationship with Kathy. I envied him for it, finding the type of love that made him want to be a better man."

"I suppose the witness protection life kind

of messes things up," she said. "Finding love, and stuff like that."

"Yeah. Hard to build a relationship on lies."

She rolled her eyes. "Don't I know it."

He risked it. "Thinking about your ex?" He paused. "I remember you told me one time about how you'd never name your child Brad because of some old baggage you carried around."

"You have a good memory."

He lifted a shoulder. "Obviously his name didn't bring back any warm fuzzy feelings for you."

"That was a big life lesson. I trusted Brad with every fiber of my being. I'm like that I guess. In for a penny and a pound and everything in between. He dated me only to use me. After he stole my work, I resolved to keep to my family, and I convinced myself that's what God wanted me to do. I have invested all my time and energy in the Dukes and done a great job keeping everyone else at arm's length." She drank some chocolate milk. "You can make your family an idol. I didn't realize that until I stepped in to help you."

He could only stare. She'd had every reason to keep him and the kids out of her life after her trust had been broken, but she stepped in, instead of away. To have that kind of maturity, courage—it floored him.

"Why are you looking at me like that?" Willow said, her cheeks flushing the pink of a desert sunrise.

"I never met someone who would put so much on the line for others."

"I have," she said softly. "You."

He didn't look away this time, the light hitting her face just so, infusing her expression with such sincerity it made him breathless. He saw respect there, for him and it made him want to preserve the moment forever.

"You've gotten through it one day at a time, alone," she said, "holding on to God's provision. That is strength, Tony. That's love."

Love. The four letters circled through his mind. "It's been a rocky path," he said slowly. "At first, I was resentful that my life was upended, that I'd been turned into a parent because of my brother. But now..." He struggled for the words. "Since Bee and Carter, my heart got bigger. The kids made that happen. They needed me to be unselfish and so I became more that way." He sighed. "God grew me so I could take care of them, or maybe He plopped them in my life to teach me who I'm meant to be. I'm not sure I'm smart enough to figure it out. It's still so hard that some days I'm sure I can't take any more learning."

She laughed softly, a sweet and inviting sound that made him smile back. He reached out, his fingertip tracing the soft skin of her hand. "Willow, forget about Brad. The baggage should be his, not yours. You deserve someone fantastic, a partner who will help you be all God wants you to be."

For a split second, he wished with all his heart that he could be that man. But she was here because she was a woman of honor who couldn't walk away from someone who needed help. It was his desperation that had brought her to him and kept her there, not devotion. He had no idea if he would ever be able to resume his normal life, let alone marry. Still, he allowed himself the tantalizing thought.

If the plan worked and Gaudy was put away...

Ron reclaimed his children...

Tony was free to be Anthony, forest service pilot...free to love whomever he wished without endangering them.

That was dangerous thinking. He pushed back his chair and stood, fiddling with his balled-up napkin. He walked a few paces away from the table, from the beautiful, valiant woman who'd risked everything for him and the children.

She stood too and then she stepped close to embrace him, pressing a featherlight kiss to his temple, which he felt deep in his heart.

"Be careful tomorrow, Tony. The kids need you."

Did she need him too? He resisted the urge to wrap her in his arms and hold her close. This wasn't that kind of kiss.

There's no room for daydreaming right now.

"Good night, Willow," he said as she headed out of the kitchen, but she was too far away to hear.

TWELVE

Diaz picked him up at six thirty Monday morning. They'd be in position well before the meet. Tony would be the lure and when they saw Ron, Diaz would move in. A trap to ensnare his brother? The notion burned.

"We can't take him unless he consents," Diaz said. "That will be your job to persuade him."

"Oh great," Tony grumbled. "That should be a piece of cake. He's already going to be angry that I didn't bring the kids."

"You'll convince him. You have to."

Tony watched the highway roll by as they headed southwest to the Rhyolite ruins. Spring had painted pockets of the neutral-toned landscape with bright pops of wildflowers, which would be gone all too soon. He had a sudden picture of himself presenting a bouquet of gorgeous flowers to Willow, imagining her joyful grin as she buried her freckled nose into the petals. His own fancies disturbed him.

Willow isn't yours and she's not ever going to be, he chided himself. Even if Ron decided to cooperate, that wasn't going to change one important fact. She was helping for the sake of the children, not because of any deep affection for him. *The kids need you*, she'd told him over chocolate milk and peanut butter and banana sandwiches. That said it all, didn't it? His life was now about children's needs, not his own desires. Unfair, but unavoidably true.

Rhyolite came into view, bathed in early light that teased silver and gold from the rocky landscape. He'd had a crash course on the defunct mining town plopped in the Bullfrog Hills near the eastern edge of Death Valley National Park. It was the typical boom to bust story of a gold supply that had dried up and the community along with it. Now the brick ruins jutted up against the sky, the only intact structures the fenced-off railway station and an odd little house made almost entirely out of glass bottles.

The area behind the railway station was their target, a broad, flat expanse of low bushes, Joshua trees and numerous signs declaring the presence of snakes. Ironic, since Gaudy, the most venomous snake of them all, had pushed them to such drastic measures.

Diaz parked her car behind the station so it was not visible from the road. Another officer rolled up in Tony's rental car. Tony hadn't liked leaving Willow, but Levi had promised to go over with his truck as soon as he tended to his horses and stay until Tony returned. That eased Tony's mind, since he was still not completely comfortable with Uncle Gino, but Severe was also patrolling the airstrip and the alarm system he'd installed himself on the front door had been engaged. It had a panic button too, that would immediately dial both Diaz and the local police. Throughout the drive, Diaz hammered him with the plan. Try to convince Ron. If necessary, get him into the car and off the premises. Press him for the evidence. Above all, don't let him bolt.

Tony waved off Diaz. "I got it. I know what I'm supposed to do."

She started to reply, but he was finished. He got out of her vehicle, trudged through the sultry heat to his car and sat in the driver's seat, air conditioner cranked. The cop stayed crouched in the back, no conversation, which suited Tony. He stretched his neck, trying to relax, still feeling the remnants of the migraine lingering deep in his left eye socket. The minutes ticked on.

Ron would likely not be on time even for his funeral, so Tony did not hold much hope that he would meet the ten-o'clock deadline. They sat silent in the car as the agonizing moments crept on. Even with the air on, it gradually became too hot. Ten o'clock, ten fifteen, ten twenty. Possibilities crowded his brain. Ron had been captured. He was already dead. He'd been scared and bolted, missing the meet. He...

His phone trilled. Diaz. "Where is your...?" she started and stopped abruptly. "Car's approaching. Compact, single driver, male."

Show time. He tensed, resisting the urge to wipe the sweat from his brow. This was going to require all his powers of persuasion, and he needed to appear in control, though his nerves were jumping like fleas on a hound dog. The officer hunkered down in the backseat.

The car stopped a couple yards away from Tony's parked car.

Now or never. "Ron," Tony said, turning off the engine and climbing out.

Ron smiled. He looked thin, haggard, but the wide grin hadn't changed since their childhood. His gaze darted around, the smile faltering. "Where are the kids?"

"I couldn't bring them. It wasn't safe."

Ron's hands went to his hips. "I want my kids, Tony."

"I know. We can make that happen, but not when you're on Gaudy's hit list."

He could see sweat glistening on Ron's forehead. "I'm getting out of here. I sent Gaudy a message last night with my account number and a small taste of what's on the thumb drive. He'll pay up. All I need to do is lay low with the kids in Mexico until the transfer is made." His look went sly. "Two million. I'm going to send some to you, bro. To thank you for helping me."

Tony felt like shaking his brother. "Gaudy isn't going to pay you two million dollars, Ron. Why would he? He has the best lawyers, a guy ready to murder for him..."

"Because I have info, passwords, transaction numbers, stuff that would ruin him, anger his clientele if it got out. I can bleed him dry."

And that was really at the core of it, Tony realized. Maybe it was born from his mother's early passing, their father's continuing jail stints, but Ron wanted to prove that he was in control. "Ron, listen, please. You can manage this, I know you can, but you need the marshals to help put him away with your info."

"No," Ron snapped. "Prison isn't enough,

not anymore. I promised Kathy I'd take care of the kids, provide for them."

"Not like this. Kathy wouldn't have wanted this."

He'd said the wrong thing. Ron's expression went from pleading to stony. "Gaudy's going to pay me, help my children, especially after what he's put us all through. It's going to hurt him. I'll make sure of it."

Tony shook his head. "You know who you sound like? Gaudy."

Ron flinched. "I'm done talking with you. Where are the kids? You don't have the right to keep them from me. You're not their father. I am."

He was losing him. "You have to listen to me…" he started.

Diaz appeared from behind the building. "Ron, your brother is right. You can't blackmail a man like Gaudy. You're putting your family in the bull's-eye."

Ron shot Tony a look that skewered right into him. "You brought the cops in, huh? You betrayed me. My own brother."

Tony stepped closer, overheated and done. "I'm trying to help you. Somebody has to be the grown-up here. There are two children who need safety and security, not the promise of some phantom four million dollars. That's tainted money."

Ron shook his head. "You never trusted me. You and Uncle Gino." He spun on his heel.

"Where are you going?" Tony yelled after him.

"If you won't give me my kids, I'll find them myself, if I have to drive every acre of this desert," he shouted over his shoulder.

"Get down," Diaz yelled, her voice drowned out by a roar that vibrated the air and kicked grit up at him as he took cover behind the car. His instincts identified the whop of the rotors before his brain caught up.

The helicopter swung low, an armed man Tony didn't know standing on the skids, firing a rifle, sunglasses glinting. Bullets tore up chunks of hot ground and gouged flecks off the brick ruins. How had Gaudy known?

Tony groaned. His brother had called to arrange the meeting and Gaudy used his techno wizardry to catch a cell phone ping, sniff out a general location and bide his time. Then it was all a waiting game.

Diaz pulled her revolver and fired as did the officer, leaping from the parked car, but the shooter laid down a barrage of bullets. Diaz dove behind a railway station bench. Tony eased around the rear fender and to the driver's side as bullets plowed through the metal, trying to keep his brother in his sights. The car was dotted with holes, the side mirror nearly shot off. The helicopter zoomed lower, enveloping them all in a dust cloud of airborne sand.

As Tony risked a look, he saw a slim bespectacled man in the helicopter's open bay, staring down with hatred. The hat and glasses hid his features, but Tony didn't have to guess to know it was Gaudy himself, come to watch the assassination of his nemesis. Tony caught sight of Ron, half-crouched, a shielding arm thrown up against the grit. There was nothing between Ron and death but a scrawny limbed Joshua tree. The thin lips curled into a smile.

No weapon, no escape. The ruined side mirror dangled in Tony's line of sight and a hazy plan formed. Grabbing it, he yanked with all his power, ignoring the burning of his fingertips. Bits of jagged metal dug into his skin, but he ripped it free. Keeping as much cover as he could, he aimed the mirror directly at the pilot's position. After a few seconds, he got the angle right, harnessing the sun and blazing it like a laser beam into the pilot's eyes. The glare would be impossible to ignore, temporarily blinding. Enough, he prayed.

The reaction was almost immediate. As

he'd hoped, the helicopter pulled away, turning from the makeshift beam.

It wouldn't work for long, but it didn't have to. The sound of police sirens echoed along the drive to the Rhyolite ruins. Diaz had called in backup and the Inyo County Sheriff's Office was responding code three. Two vehicles blazed up the road.

Sunglasses guy let off a final burst of gunfire, crawled back into helicopter, and it roared off.

Tony left the protection of the vehicle, following the officer who'd taken cover there too. The cop had a small cut on his forehead but seemed none the worse for wear as did Diaz. She stood a hand on her hip, radiating fury as hot as the air as she holstered her weapon and muttered savagely.

"Gaudy outflanked us again," she snarled. "I'm getting sick and tired of this."

Tony wasn't listening. Brushing off the grit from his clothes, he tried to see through the subsiding cloud of dust. Ron and his car were gone. He'd used the sandstorm created by the helicopter and the arrival of the sheriffs to drive off the back way disappearing into the desert beyond.

Diaz grunted. "Ron is a fool if he thinks he can survive this."

He might be a fool, but he wouldn't stop trying. Tony knew his brother and he knew he'd just lost the only chance he had at changing Ron's mind.

Willow prepared apple slices and peanut butter for a midmorning snack. Carter enjoyed them, but Bee simply made a big mess. *Note to self, if you serve it, you gotta clean it.*

She wiped Bee's sticky hands, pleased that her cough was better.

Willow had received a photo via her email from the clinic. Amidst all the other chaos, she'd almost forgotten that Bee needed a breathing treatment. Her thoughts kept wandering to Tony. Had he been able to convince Ron? Had Ron even shown up in the first place? She said another silent prayer that above all, no one would be hurt.

Levi texted, Had a horse problem. On my way now. U ok?

She reassured him that she and the kids were fine and went back to her peanut butter removal. "How did you manage to get it in your hair?"

Bee aimed a toothy grin at her. "Big mess," she chortled.

"That's for sure." Six sheets of paper towels later, and the goo was vanquished.

Precisely on time, the nurse knocked on the door. Gino got to the door first, a finger to his lips. He stood out of sight, his hand on the gun holstered in his belt. Willow looked through the window to check the visitor's clipped-on badge against the info sent by the clinic. She could just make out the name lettered on the badge. A slender lady with glasses and hair plaited into a thick black braid offered a nervous wave through the window. Willow gave Gino a thumbs-up and let her in. They shook hands and exchanged names. Willow took a closer look at the nurse's badge.

"I wasn't sure I was in the right place," Inez said, jumping when she caught sight of Gino, who had at least stowed his weapon. "Oh, I didn't see you there."

Willow wished Gino's smile wasn't so much of a scowl. "Thank you for coming," she said.

"No problem. It's…an unusual location but you can find anything with a GPS."

Inez gave Uncle Gino the side-eye when his stare lingered. "Is there, um, something wrong?"

"No," Willow said, firmly. "Let me introduce you to Bee."

In the living room play area, Bee cooperatively left her brother and their blocks and toddled over to meet the nurse, Moo clenched under her arm. Bee hit it off right away with Inez, as she did everyone.

"Be back in a minute, Carter," Willow said.

Carter nodded, attention fixed on building a block tunnel for his trains.

Willow led the way to the bedroom, where the nurse hooked up her nebulizer and slid a little mask over Bee's face. Inez coughed into her elbow. "Sorry. My allergies are bad in the spring. Scratchy throat."

Willow fetched her a glass of water. Gino had vanished somewhere. She returned to find Inez pretending to make Moo Moo dance, which elicited giggles from Bee as the child inhaled the medicated steam. Willow was delighted that Bee was so cooperative. *Plucky* was a good descriptor, in spite of the setbacks. Innately resilient, but probably somewhat a credit to Tony, who had struggled to keep her safe and feeling loved.

Tony. Her heart lurched as she checked the clock. Had the meeting happened? Was he safe?

Uncle Gino poked his head in. "Everything okay?"

Inez gave Moo to Bee and began to pack her bag. "Yes," she said. "Our sweet patient is doing well. Almost done."

He gave a thumbs-up. "Going to take a stroll."

By that, Willow knew he meant he would climb the lookout tower.

Willow noticed the worry lines grooving the nurse's brow. She chewed on her lip, transferring some pink gloss to her teeth.

"Is there something wrong?" Willow asked with a flare of worry. "Is Bee not progressing fast enough?"

"No...nothing wrong. Bee's fine." Ingrid toyed with the zipper on her bag. "I'm afraid you might think I'm paranoid, but I've seen him before and he looked just as unfriendly."

"Who?"

"That man who was just here."

"Gino? Where did you see him?"

"He was talking to someone at the clinic. A bruiser of a guy." She stripped off her rubber gloves.

"When?"

"When did I see him?" She thought it over. "Last night when my shift was over." She excused herself to wash her hands in the bathroom. Willow stared after her.

Uncle Gino had met someone last night at the clinic? The minutes ticked by in a slow, silent panic. The implications of what Inez had revealed were dizzying. She was startled when the nurse returned from the bathroom.

"I'm going to head out now," Inez said. "No

offense, but it's kind of creepy here. Call if you need anything or if Bee's cough doesn't continue to improve. Otherwise I'll be back for one more treatment in two days. I'll let myself out. You stay here and try to keep Bee still for a few minutes to let the medicine work."

Scooping Bee close, Willow went to her window and watched as Inez departed, mind spinning in frantic circles. Struggling against her usual tendency to make snap decisions, she tried to think it out slowly and methodically. Uncle Gino had been talking to a man who matched Klee's description at the clinic. But he'd claimed to be driving around the airstrip and surrounding properties. The nurse could be lying, but why would she? A woman who had been dispatched by a doctor? She would have no motive to lie...but Gino?

She'd never trusted him, and she'd been right. Decision time. If she was wrong, she'd be embarrassed, but if she was right... Levi was probably already en route. She'd text him to hurry and call the cops. She had to get the kids out and away immediately.

But her phone was not in her pocket. Nor was it charging near the front door when she sprinted over to check, Bee giggling as she ran. Could someone have taken it from the charger?

Someone? Or Uncle Gino?

Was that the sound of an engine? She ran to the front window in time to see a car entering the road heading for the airstrip. It was unfamiliar, not law enforcement or her brothers, and not the nurse returning for some forgotten item.

A trap. Tony had been lured away and Uncle Gino took her phone, knowing they would be easy pickings for Klee. Where was Severe? Why hadn't he come to check on her?

Another betrayal? The car was driving fast now, kicking up a dusty trail. How could she get help?

The alarm by the front door. Though she'd disconnected it to let Inez in, she could manually trip it in a second. That would send a message directly to the police. She stabbed at the panic button.

Nothing happened. Heart in her throat she looked closer. The panel was blank. The wires leading to the unit had been yanked out, severing the electrical supply. But surely the battery backup…

Now she could see the open tab at the bottom where the battery had been removed. Willow had no idea where she might find a spare and there was no time. Nerves kindling to fire, she ran for Carter.

"Come on, Carter," she said, "we have to go now."

"Where?" he said.

Where? With Klee closing in from the front and Gino probably even closer, there was only one possible escape.

The tunnel.

THIRTEEN

Tony figured that Diaz would come up with a plan B to deal with his brother, but at the moment, Ron wasn't the top of his worry list. He'd called Willow with no answer.

Then he texted. Still nothing. A ball of ice formed in his veins at odds with the sweat that dampened his shirt. For what reason could she be out of contact? She'd taken the kids outside, she'd forgotten to charge her phone. Neither sounded likely.

He was going to ask Diaz to contact Severe, but she had her phone pressed to her ear, face grave.

A river of dread crawled up and down his spine. He was about to try messaging Uncle Gino when Diaz disconnected. "That was Levi. He found Severe unconscious from a bullet wound."

Tony froze, trying to read the message in her dark eyes. "Where?"

He saw her throat move as she swallowed. "The airstrip."

That was all Tony needed to hear. He wrenched open the bullet-pocked door.

Diaz reached to stop him, palms slapping the hood, but he gunned the engine and peeled out.

"Tony, don't do this," she yelled.

He didn't slow. They'd have to handcuff him to prevent him from going. Clutching the steering wheel with all his strength was not enough to keep away the terrible "what ifs" that blasted through his brain.

He thought he'd known fear in his life. On one occasion he'd flown through skies thick with impenetrable smoke and instruments malfunctioning. Blind and expecting to see an obstacle materialize in front of him at any second, he was not sure he would survive. And the moment he'd thought he'd lost Carter in the shoe store, clutching Bee and shouting for the boy in a near frenzied state until he spotted him at the drinking fountain near the employee break room.

Now the feeling that seized him was pure white-hot terror unlike he'd ever known. What would he find at the airstrip? Willow? The children? Gone? Hurt? Or worse? The smart thing would have been to ask more questions of Diaz, to go with them and wait while they secured the building, but his overriding fear would not allow it. Urgency roared through him and kept his foot pressed to the accelerator, pebbles pinging a frantic rhythm under his tires.

He made the drive much faster than he should have, careening onto the road to find an ambulance tending to the stricken Severe. The officer moved an arm as they loaded him onto the stretcher so Tony was able to ascertain that he was alive as he flew by. He sent up a quick prayer of thanks that Severe hadn't been murdered.

Levi's truck was at the house, the driver's door open. Another vehicle was there too, probably Klee's. Uncle Gino and Levi stood just inside the doorway glaring at each other. Levi's rifle was over his shoulder.

"Where's my sister? The kids?" Levi shouted.

"I told you I don't know," Gino shouted back. His cheeks were blotched red and his breath came in gasps. "I was up in the tower and I saw Klee rolling onto the property. He shot Severe." He panted. "I ran back down and he got a bead on me, pinned me inside. I returned fire, but he outgunned me. By the time I made it in, they were gone, the alarm disabled. Batteries missing too."

Tony sprinted to the bedrooms. The closets, under the beds, maybe they'd hidden.

"I already checked," Levi said, catching up to him. "She's not here. But there's…" He let the sentence trail off. Tony stopped and turned.

"There's no blood," Levi finished quietly.

No blood. Time staggered to a full stop. They were okay, they had to be. Willow… Bee… Carter. But what if they weren't? Everything in his world had suddenly vanished. He would not, could not accept it.

There was one hope left.

"The tunnel," he said, more to himself than Levi. Willow was smart, savvy, she would have headed for the tunnel at the first hint of trouble like they'd practiced. She was safe there with the kids, she had to be.

"Wait for the cops," he shouted to Uncle Gino.

He and Levi pounded down the hallway into the back storage room and flung up the trapdoor. Tony was poised to shout into the darkness when Levi stopped him. "If Klee's down there he'll get you with one shot."

Tony closed his mouth, jaws grinding together. "This could be bad," he said.

"Yeah," Levi agreed.

They exchanged a long look, understanding passing between them. There was no point in speaking further. Neither would flinch from whatever lay below, not if it could help save the kids and Willow.

Levi loved his sister.

At that moment, something in Tony's chest felt very much like love too, but there was no time to think it over.

"Text Diaz. You won't get a signal once we're in." Levi elbowed him out of the way before he slung his rifle over his shoulder and climbed down. Tony dashed off a message and without waiting for a reply, followed.

Hang on, Willow. Just hang on.

Willow had strapped on the headlamp from the backpack Austin left on her first time down the ladder, while the kids stayed at the top. Two times more she'd gone up and down the ladder to fetch Bee and then Carter. Sweat trickled down her back from the effort. Now the cold air chilled her as they followed the glowing paint signals. The headlamp punched small holes into the gloom, enough for her to guide them slowly along on a "treasure hunt" as she'd tried to present it. The story was weak and unconvincing even to herself. Carter's hand was shaking in her own and Bee's eyes were huge in the darkness. Willow wished she'd grabbed jackets for the kids but there had been no chance, with Uncle Gino unaccounted for and Klee approaching the front door. Bee whimpered.

"It's okay, sweetie," Willow said. "We'll be out of here in a few more minutes."

She stopped. Had she heard something? Ears straining she caught the sound of dripping water, possibly the scrabbling claws of some rodent visitor. Normal noises for an undisturbed tunnel. Steeling her spine, she kept going. Three more steps and she stopped again as a thunk sounded somewhere behind them. Was it Gino? Klee? Levi come to find her? The possibilities paralyzed her as she clutched the children close, trying to decide what to do.

"Hey," a voice shouted down the tunnel, echoing off the narrow walls. She jerked involuntarily, causing Bee to drop Moo. It wasn't Gino, but it was surely not Tony or Levi either. Fear almost choked her. She flicked off her headlamp and stayed quiet.

"Quit running," the voice said, floating along the dark confines of the tunnel. "I ain't getting paid enough to chase you. There's no point in it and I about busted my head on a rock just now. Gonna catch up anyways, so why bother? The kiddies might get hurt."

Klee. How had he found the tunnel entrance? Her lungs refused to work. Slowly she knelt to Carter and put her finger to his lips. He understood, but there was no guarantee the Bee would remain quiet. How far behind was Klee? She knew tunnels could funnel sound and make it hard to discern the answer. There was no way back, only forward.

Moving as silently as she could, she hurried them along, hoping she was sticking to the painted path. At the exit, she would land in a broad stretch of nowhere in deadly heat, but her chances of running to the main road or hiding until Levi or Tony found them was better than what she faced with Klee in an enclosed tunnel.

"Oww," Klee said again. "I mean it, lady. I gotta turn the girl over to Gaudy, but the boy's mine and I don't want him damaged so quit running right now."

To emphasize the point, he fired a shot, which sparked off the rock walls, ricocheting wildly. Barely containing her scream, she dropped to the floor, covering Carter and Bee as best she could. The missile sparked and clanged as it zinged from surface to surface until it finally came to rest somewhere beyond them. What kind of a dope shot into a confined space?

Her breath sounded loud in her own ears and she could feel Bee winding up to wail.

Carter was crying too. She couldn't see him but she felt his silent heaving as she climbed to her feet. "Shhhhhh," she whispered. "Take care of Moo, okay?" When she decided no more shots were coming for the moment, she tugged Carter and Bee along the paint trail. "We'll keep going," she whispered. "We're almost out."

Were they? She thought so but time was distorted by her fear. Their steps weren't silent, and she wondered if Klee could even hear her raspy breathing.

He was closer, his footsteps louder. "Carter's a weird name for a boy. I'm going to call him Jeff, after my father." Klee's words sliced into her. He was probably only a few yards distant, and she heard no other sounds that someone was coming to save them.

"These paint dots are handy," he said. "They're leading me right to you."

Tears blurred her vision as she continued on, knowing it was futile. By her estimation there was still another quarter mile left until the exit at least, and he would catch up within minutes. They drew even with an offshoot tunnel, stretching into tarry blackness. She shielded the headlamp with her shirt and activated it. She could see only a cramped passage, strewn with rocks that must have fallen from above. She recalled what Austin had said.

These tunnels go on for miles in all directions and much of it is on the brink of collapse. You'd be a fool to go exploring.

But she'd be a fool to let Klee chase her down, probably kill her and certainly take the children. She'd be more than a fool, she'd be a quitter.

Willow felt that stubborn Duke blood rise up in her veins. She'd failed at many things, but she would not give up on these children until her last heartbeat faded away. As silently as she could, she doused the light, removed one of Bee's pink shoes and flung it as far along the marked path as she could. Then she backtracked the few steps to the offshoot passageway her brother had warned her about.

"All right, you two," she whispered to the kids. "We're going to play a game of hide and seek until Uncle Tony finds us." *Please God, help us survive this.* Bee clutched to her hip, and holding tight to Carter's hand, Willow led them into the abyss.

"Quit running now…" came the voice echoing down the corridor.

Tony couldn't catch all of Klee's words, but he knew from the timbre of the voice who it belonged to. It was enough to send Levi and Tony scrambling forward so quickly that Tony banged his head on a projection of rock, biting back the cry of pain.

They moved quickly, considering they had only their phone flashlights and the glow marks to light their way.

Suddenly, Levi stopped him with a fist to the chest. "He's right up ahead, near the old ore car. I'm not going to fire unless I see Willow and the kids aren't in harm's way. I need a clean shot."

"Give me two minutes."

Levi didn't ask, merely nodded and crept as close as he could while staying behind a covering rock.

Tony dropped to his belly, the cold seeping straight through his T-shirt. He crawled slowly and methodically, inching his way around the pinch in the tunnel and into the widened space, where he saw Klee, gun in hand, examining the area with a small penlight. Tony could not detect Willow and the kids. Klee's actions betrayed that he was still searching for them too.

That brought Tony a small measure of relief. His fingers closed around the nearest loose rock. He didn't trust himself to deliver the same fantastic pitch that had broken the light in the garage, but at least it would allow Levi to move into a safer range where he would not risk hitting Willow or the kids if they were also crouched in the darkness.

He let loose the rock, sidearm style, and it struck Klee in the shoulder. He whirled around as Levi stepped in. Tony scrambled upright.

"Stop right there," Levi shouted. "Not safe to shoot here, but I'll risk it if I have to."

Klee raised his hands, but the gun stayed in his right, the penlight in his left. He smiled. "I like this tunnel setup. Good to have an emergency escape, right? And a neato adventure for my boy."

"Where are Willow and the kids?" Tony demanded.

Klee laughed. "You've lost track of them? I won't let that happen when little Jeffie is mine. I'm gonna be a good parent."

He'd picked out a new name for Carter? Tony fought down the fury. "You're not going to touch him," he growled, fighting to get the words out. He turned on his phone light and played it over the dark crannies. They had to be there somewhere. "How did you know about the tunnel?" he said, as he searched.

Klee laughed. "Now that'd be telling." He laughed once more and flicked off his penlight. At the same time he blasted off two quick shots. Tony hit the ground again as the bullets bounced off the walls and tore through the darkness.

Levi took cover as well.

Tony's ears rang with the percussive blasts until the bullet eventually lost momentum. As his head cleared he heard a more ominous sound, a rumbling from below. His fingertips detected movement in the damp rock pressed to his belly.

"Levi," he shouted, but an enormous chunk of rock was already breaking away from overhead. With a massive roar it slammed into the ground an inch from Tony's shoulder. He rolled in the other direction, mashing himself against the clammy wall. The floor vibrated with the force of the impact.

Was the whole tunnel collapsing? Had Willow and the kids found shelter? He hadn't finished the thought when the trembling subsided. Gasping for breath, he sprang to his feet, muddy and scraped.

Levi emerged from his shadowy corner, rifle aimed as he peered around the fallen rock.

"He's gone," Levi said. "Headed for the exit."

"Let him go. We have to find Willow and the kids."

They surged over the rock-strewn ground, avoiding obstacles as best they could. Maneuvering around a puddle, a flash of color stood out in the beam of his light. He bent, picking up a small pink shoe.

He locked eyes with Levi. "She headed to the exit," Levi said. "Maybe she got out before we intercepted Klee."

Maybe. He considered that, walking backward a few paces where he felt a crosscurrent of air that emanated from behind an opening crudely barred with wood slats and a keep out sign.

It was possible she'd run ahead.

Or perhaps she'd realized she could not beat Klee and decided to hide, the shoe left as a diversion.

Levi appeared to read his thoughts. "I'll go to the exit. You check out the tunnel. Don't go far in."

Tony nodded as Levi disappeared in pursuit of Klee. He looked closer at the wood slats nailed over the small entrance. It would be a tight squeeze for his six-foot frame, but no problem for a slender woman and two small kids.

If he was wrong, he was wasting time, leaving Levi without a wingman, and possibly endangering his own life. But if he was right?

What did he know about Willow?

That she was creative, tenacious, with a

courage that left him breathless. Had she gone for the exit, a sure escape if the timing was right?

Or created a diversion, relying on her own wits to buy time?

One thing was certain. She wouldn't avoid risking herself to keep the children safe from Klee.

All right, Willow. I'm on my way.

FOURTEEN

Willow had barely bitten back her scream at the gunshots. Her pulse was still roaring as she squeezed farther along the side tunnel. Was Klee firing indiscriminately? But wouldn't that risk the boy he wanted to take? The floor rumbled again underneath her feet, and she worried another rock might fall as it had a moment before.

She had to get away. Just far enough to hide but not so far that she could not find her way back once the coast was clear.

She led Carter along the downward-pitched tunnel. It pinched close, requiring them to duck down to enter a small flatter cavern, buttressed by wooden beams. There were other remnants of mining activity, a wooden crate, a pile of rusted nails. If only those long-ago miners had left a candle or lantern behind. Her headlamp hardly made a dent in the inky black. She did her best to examine the space.

The cavern had only one other exit, a passageway slightly bigger than Bee and littered with rock debris. It was all but impassable, and she was loathe to go any farther from the main tunnel anyway.

"All right," she told Carter and Bee. "We'll stay here for a little while and then we'll go back to the house. Okay?"

"Where's Uncle Tony?" Carter said. He was too scared to remember the lie he'd been taught about referring to Tony as his daddy.

"I'm sure he's coming soon," she said.

Carter's expression was stark. He looked at his sneakers and held one up for closer inspection. It was wet. She had not realized the floor was damp.

"Up you go." She hoisted Carter up onto the box, where he sat with his feet dangling over the side. Resting Bee next to him, she strained to hear any sounds beyond a soft murmur, which she took to be wind blowing in from a faraway fissure. She opened the backpack, relieved to find a flashlight and extra batteries.

"So we can see our way out," she said brightly. Bee coughed, and Willow pulled out a tightly folded silver emergency blanket, the metallic sheen reflected in Bee's eager gaze She spread it around both kids and showed Carter how to hold it in his hands to secure it.

"Like a cape," she said. "Neat, right?"

How long was she going to be able to keep the kids from recognizing her true feelings? With no phone and no watch, she was not at all sure how much time had passed since the shots. Five minutes? Fifteen?

With a gasp, she finally noticed that her own feet were chilled, her sneakers soggy and her ankles as well. How had she not noticed the water when they came in? At least the kids were okay at the moment, safe on their wooden perch.

Five minutes, she decided. Maybe ten, and then she'd lead them back into the main tunnel. To head back to the house seemed a safer idea, since hopefully she'd lured Klee toward the exit with Bee's shoe.

She tried to keep count of the seconds in her head.

One thousand one, one thousand two… There was another vibration under her feet, the rock resettling itself. She tensed. *Please, God, not an earthquake, not now.*

A scrap of dried wood floated past her foot. There hadn't been that much water a moment before, had there? As she watched, the water inched to the top of her sock. Terrified, she realized the tunnel was flooding.

"Kids…" she said, moving toward them. A

footstep from the outer tunnel immobilized her. Klee was coming. *What do I do?* She looked frantically around. Maybe they could hide in the tiny passageway? But the water was pouring in now, up to her shin, ice-cold. They would drown.

"No, no," Bee cried, shoving off the silver blanket. She wanted to look down into the swirling water.

"Quiet, Bee, please," Willow said urgently, but as Carter struggled to hold the blanket, she knew Bee would not be placated this time. A weapon was her only hope against the intruder. She swept up a broken board and put herself between the children and the entrance. Frigid water lapped at her thighs now as she raised the board. Tears started up but she blinked them away.

"You have to be strong," she scolded herself. She'd probably only get one swing to surprise Klee before he squeezed off a shot. Wood slivers bit into her fingers as she clutched the flimsy weapon.

Behind her, Bee struggled with her brother. "Nooooooo," she said, her toddler complaint loud as a struck gong in the cramped space. The movement outside stopped. Hardly able to hold on to the board, she willed herself to push away the cold, the fear, and focus on giving them one last chance to survive.

"Bee," a deep voice shouted. "Willow, Carter. Where are you?"

Elation replaced the terror. As Willow dropped the piece of wood, she thought she'd never been so happy to hear another human voice. "Tony, we're in here," she called out.

Tony sloshed into the cavern. He swept her up into a fierce embrace, whispering in her ear, "Thank God. Thank God."

She hugged him back, tearstained face pressed into his neck. "You found us."

He clung to her for one more long minute, kissing her on both cheeks and the forehead before he eased her back. "Water's filling this level. We have to get out of here."

She grabbed the backpack and Tony shouldered it. "Is Klee still out there?"

"Levi's tracking him to the exit. I think he fell for your shoe diversion."

"I'm glad you didn't."

He chuckled as he hoisted Bee, who was writhing in irritation. "I would never lose track of you, Willow."

There were way too many feelings to process about that loaded statement, so she settled on cramming the blanket into the pack and inviting Carter onto her back. "Piggy back ride?"

"Are we going back to the house?" Carter asked as he clasped her around the neck and waist. "I'm cold."

"Yes," she said through chattering teeth. "We sure are. I am ready for a hot shower, how about you?"

"Uh-huh," he said. She activated the head-lamp, which confirmed that the water had risen to her belt level, though it hit Tony just above the knees. They squeezed out of the cavern and into the sloped tunnel. Splashes and gurgles nearly deafened them. There was a strong current that seemed intent on tugging her into the darkness, but she lowered her chin and fought along in Tony's wake. He held Bee to his hip and reached a hand to Willow, taking her elbow to keep him next to her.

That touch seemed to push away the fear and the chill and made the going easier. Bee still wriggled against Tony.

"Sorry, angel. You can't get down right now."

Willow stumbled on the uneven corridor, but Tony's grip kept her upright.

"Only a few more feet and we'll be back in the upper tunnel," he said.

She plowed on, Carter's arms tight against her throat. "Let go a little bit, okay, Carter?"

He eased his clutch slightly. Her limbs were

going numb, but she resisted the urge to ask Tony how much farther he thought it would be.

One foot in front of the other until you get out of this mess, she told herself as the water continued to fight against her.

Tony's mind spun as he forged ahead along the corridor, trying to put together next steps. There were too many possibilities. Klee could have eluded Levi and was heading back in their direction. It was possible he had alerted his people and Levi had walked into a trap at the exit point, but there was no way to warn him.

His phone was still functioning since it was still dry in his breast pocket. He sent a text to Levi but got the endless "sending" message. There was zero chance he could get a call out from this deep underground. Diaz must have found the tunnel trapdoor or she'd contact Austin, who would tell her about it. Police were on their way. Weren't they?

Doubts dripped down on him in a smothering curtain. He'd assumed Gaudy had found their meet with Ron when he tracked his phone. But Klee had known when to attack the airstrip. How? Severe? And then he'd been shot by his accomplice? Possible, but not likely. Uncle Gino? He still couldn't make himself believe it. Diaz? Was Gaudy paying her to find Ron? The chill numbed him and he could feel Bee shivering, but he didn't dare stop to wrap the emergency blanket around her.

Best to get out of the flood, assess the tunnel situation and head back to the trapdoor. Surely the place was swarming with cops who might even be heading their way at that very moment.

Willow's body was rigid with cold and he tried to tuck her closer to transfer whatever body warmth he had left. Tough as she was, she was beginning to slow, each step an effort.

"Let me carry Carter too," he said. "You can hold on to my belt."

"Carter's not heavy, and he's keeping a lookout. He's such a helper." Willow patted the boy's leg, but Carter didn't answer. Something under the surface caused her to stumble.

He felt her slip from his grasp with a soft cry. Flailing, he lunged to catch her but the water sucked her away from his seeking fingers. In horror, he saw her pinwheel one arm while the other clutched Carter's leg in a death grip.

Carter's expression was frozen in shock, a small pool of pale skin against the black.

Tony threw out his hand and tried again to grab for Willow and Carter but they disappeared under the eddies. Yelling, reeling, panicked, he staggered after them, clipping his shoulder on a rock. His phone flashlight shook in his hands as he searched. A few feet away he thought he caught the glimmer of her hair. He charged toward it, one arm clutched tight as he tried to keep Bee from slipping too. The suction pulled and dragged him, and Bee's cries were muffled in the roar. *Follow the current, find them. Save them.*

"Willow," he shouted, scanning the darkness for any sign of them. Mist from the splashing water dazzled his vision, Bee's wailing mixing with the echoes until his brain threatened to explode. Was that an arm? He shoved the phone in his pocket, dove forward and reached out, lunging at nothing.

Despair licked at him as the minutes ticked past. He staggered in frantic circles with no sign of them until...

There. A glimmer of yellow light shone a few yards ahead of him.

The faint glow lit hope inside him. It must be her headlamp. With renewed energy, he fought his way along. Bee's cries had morphed into shrieks, her sobs stabbing his ears. Reaching the dim light, he thrust his hand out blindly. At first, he felt nothing but the stone wall. Splashing in wild arcs, he was barely able to keep his hold on Bee. At long last, his fingers brushed something soft and yielding. He saw the barest glimpse of two faces peering at him. Willow clung to a section of iron pipe that she'd somehow grasped with a fist while holding on to Carter's wrist with the other. Water foamed and thundered around them. Her white-knuckled grip was the only thing keeping them from being swept away.

With a huge effort, he grabbed her wrist and pulled them to him. It took all his strength to fight the current without letting go of Bee. Willow seemed to be suspended there, his strength not enough to pull her closer. Bee's weight was tugging him the other way. His body screamed for him to let go. To lose Bee? To give up on Willow and Carter?

That was a hard no. Fighting for breath and against his cramping muscles, he summoned the strength for one more heave. The sinew-snapping effort was just enough to break the grasp of the current, allowing him to haul Willow and Carter to his chest. Her headlamp tumbled away into the foam. They all clung together for a moment, him panting, Willow and Carter coughing, Bee sobbing. All beautiful noises to Tony for what they represented.

Life. Another chance.

The water had leveled off at his waist, which meant it was almost to Willow's nose and Carter's chin as she managed to hold him above the water level. He took Carter and put him up on his shoulders, Bee against his chest, tied there with the emergency blanket from the backpack. Carter was shivering violently, but he clasped icy fingers around Tony's neck. Bee was shivering now too, no longer crying which scared him. Willow didn't resist when he drew her firmly to his side. "See?" He panted. "Told you I'd never lose you."

She heaved in a breath and tried to answer, but no words came out.

"Together," he said. "We go together from here on out."

She leaned against him, coughing.

Some how he kept pushing on, towing them along as if he was a tugboat, until the tunnel sloped up to deliver them from the water. His body begged for rest, but he did not think he would be able to start again once he stopped so they plowed on for an eternity, finally reaching the main tunnel and crawling out through the wooden slats.

The sound of scuffling feet made him pull them all back into the shadows, and a light blazed into their faces, blinding them.

"US Marshals," Diaz called. "Hands up."

"We're the people you're supposed to be protecting," Tony said through chattering teeth. He identified them, and Diaz lowered the light.

"Where's my brother?" Willow said.

"He's fine. We had to physically restrain him from going back in the tunnel to search once we ascertained Klee had left the area. He's back at the house. Can you walk?" She directed another officer to help carry the kids, but Tony shook his head.

"No one," he spat, "is going to touch these children unless I say so."

Diaz raised her palm in surrender, and they made their way as fast as they could to the ladder. Austin and Levi peered anxiously from the top.

Elbowing a cop out of the way, they both scrambled down. Austin took Carter and climbed up, even though it was likely a challenge with his weakened shoulder. Levi helped Willow, and Tony retied the silver blanket around him to tether Bee closer as he made his way painfully up, his shoulders and strained muscles in his arm complaining at each rung. In time to the throbbing, his soul quietly said a thank-you that every step brought Willow and the children closer to the safety they deserved.

Willow refused the care of the doctor the police had summoned to the airstrip. Doc Howley set to work checking the children after they'd been bundled into dry clothes and given mugs of hot cocoa. Tony watched the doctor's every move.

"No harm done, it seems. She's got a bit of wheezing still," Doc Howley said. "I'll order a decongestant. You can pick them up at the pharmacy in town this afternoon."

"We'll send someone," Diaz said.

Bee fell promptly asleep in the cot, and Carter climbed in next to her with the borrowed train toy in his grasp. Moo had only gotten slightly damp, somehow, and Bee stuffed it under her chin before she'd conked out.

When Willow was reasonably sure they were okay, she allowed Levi to propel her toward the bathroom. "Take a shower and warm up. I'll bring some clothes and drop them inside the door."

She didn't have the energy to argue. The hot water did not penetrate for several minutes, but eventually it eased away the chill that had invaded her bones. For the first time she allowed herself to feel the fear she'd kept at bay. Tears streamed down her face and she sank to the floor of the shower, unable even to turn off the water as it eventually ran cold. Nor did she acknowledge the tap on the door when Mara entered. Her voice, her body, her mind, were in a state of dysfunction.

Wordlessly, Mara took in Willow's sorry condition, grabbed a towel and brought it over. "You were a champion," Mara said quietly. "And however you're feeling is okay."

Willow tried to answer, to smile, but all she could do was cry. Mara helped her up and toweled her off, guiding her into pajamas and a robe. *But I have to get dressed*, she tried to say, *to go help with the kids*.

Instead, she allowed herself to be shepherded like a child into the hallway, where Tony stood in dry clothes, arms crossed and pensive. He jerked when he saw her. "Is she…" He looked at Mara and then at Willow. "Are you okay?"

Willow managed a nod.

"She needs to rest for a while," Mara said.

Tony didn't take his gaze off her. "Diaz wants to talk to her, but I don't care. In here," he said, pushing the door open to the little bedroom. "The children are sleeping together so there's a free cot. That way I can keep watch over all of you at once."

Uncle Gino… she thought. *I have to tell him about Uncle Gino.* But her mouth simply wouldn't work. She climbed in and it was

Tony who pulled the covers up to her chin and kissed her forehead.

"We can't trust Gino," she mumbled.

"I'll take care of it." He dropped a second kiss on her cheek and let his lips rest there for a moment. "You are the bravest person I have ever known," he murmured. "And no matter how long I live I will never be able to thank you enough."

Drifting away, she let herself rest in the comfort of the warm blankets, the sense of safety, the trembling sincerity in Tony's words.

She snapped awake several hours later, uncertain, groggy. Tony was moving quietly around the room, shoving things into a duffel bag. There was someone else talking too.

"Bad idea…"

"Quiet," he snarled. "Don't wake them up."

"Too late," Willow said, sitting up and taking in the angry tableau of Diaz and Uncle Gino.

Tony huffed out a breath. "Sorry, Willow." He pointed to the sleeping children and said to Diaz, "At least let's go into the living room so you don't wake them up too."

Diaz and Gino led the way. Feeling foolish in her robe and slippers, Willow took Tony's outstretched hand, suddenly recalling what she'd needed to tell him. "Tony, the nurse said Uncle Gino was talking to a man like Klee at the clinic," she whispered. "He could be…"

He looped an arm around her shoulders. "I figured there was a reason you didn't try to get to Uncle Gino for help instead of choosing the tunnel. I mentioned it to your brothers already. I've got a plan. Follow my lead."

Levi and Austin were in chairs. They both broke into identical smiles when she settled herself on the sofa, rising to drop a kiss on each of her cheeks.

"Willow Duke, cave master," Austin said, but his kidding tone didn't quiet reach his eyes. "Let's not do that again, anytime soon, though, right?"

"Severe is going to pull through," Diaz said. "He's still under sedation, but he's out of surgery. Tell us what happened, Willow."

They listened as Willow related her story. She lifted her chin and looked right at Gino when she told about the nurse seeing Gino at the clinic.

"Those are lies," Gino said. "The nurse made it up. I told Diaz as much."

"Why would she?" Levi said.

"Hold up," Diaz said. "I heard what Tony had to say already. We'll check on the nurse, and we've got a fingerprint team coming to dust the alarm. We'll check and see if there are any witnesses putting Gino at the clinic."

It took Willow a moment to process. Inez, the nurse, was a suspect? But she'd been referred by the clinic, wore an ID badge and been wary of Gino. Had it been an act? She replayed the events in her mind. Had Inez had time to disable the alarm? The answer was yes, since she'd let herself out while Willow settled Bee. Willow chewed her lip. Was it possible she'd been wrong about everything? Gaudy could certainly hire anyone he wanted, paying a nurse to do his bidding would be easily accomplished. It had been a woman who called the Furnace Falls clinic to try and get information about Tony. Faking her badge was child's play for a man like Gaudy.

Levi leaned forward, elbows on his knees, snagging her attention. "We called Jude. He's cut his training short and he's got a red-eye flight. He'll be back tomorrow."

Willow felt dizzy with relief.

"We don't need…" Diaz started.

"Don't need what?" Tony challenged. "The local sheriff butting in? I think that's exactly what we need since this place is no longer secure."

He took Willow's hand. "With your permission," he said to her, "I want to take you and the kids someplace safe for the night, until your cousin Jude makes it here."

"No way," Diaz said. "That's a ridiculous idea."

"Ridiculous would be staying here and letting Klee or Gaudy waltz right in for another go."

"Fine. We'll get you on a flight somewhere else or drive you there."

"No offense, but I can't trust you," Tony said. "Or you," he added with a glance at Gino. "I don't know where my brother is and he's not going to cooperate with you anyway, so it seems like your plan didn't work. I'm sorry. I truly hoped he would help put Gaudy away. Right now, I can't fix any of that. I'm going to keep Willow and the kids alive and pray that Jude can help us figure out a long-term solution." He handed her his cell phone. "And Levi got me a satellite burner phone, so you won't be able to track me using this."

Diaz snatched the phone. "Where do you think you'll find a safe spot? Huh? Gaudy can find you anywhere. We're your only protection."

"Sorry if I don't see it that way, in light of what happened." Tony's eyes were ablaze. "Willow is the only reason Bee and Carter are here right now so your protection isn't working." He squeezed her fingers. "I have a place we can go, until tomorrow when Jude arrives, but... I understand if you want to stay here, with your family."

Her family. Her rock. Her safety. But her heart thrummed with a new pulse and she realized that she was beginning to feel like Carter, Bee and Tony were her family too.

With a sinking heart, she knew she was lying to herself. Not family. Not really. There was only a deep friendship between them.

Well, if that's what God meant for her to be for Tony, so be it. She would see it through, until they didn't need her anymore.

"I'm in," she said.

He exhaled long and slow. "We'll let the kids rest."

"And we'll load you up on supplies," Austin said.

Diaz's expression was thunderous. "So this supposedly secure location is a Duke family secret? Law enforcement isn't to be trusted but locals know everything?"

"Not all locals," Austin said. "Just a select few." He ignored her fuming and got to his feet. "I'll get started on a few things. Levi will keep watch here until departure time."

Uncle Gino shook his head. "This is the

wrong choice. The only way we can stop this is to get Ron," he said.

Willow wasn't sure who he was talking to.

"Even if you get him, you can't make him cooperate," Tony said.

"Maybe you can't, but I can." The steel line of Gino's mouth awakened a ripple of unease in Willow's belly. He was planning something.

Whatever it was, she hoped Tony and the kids were far away from the fallout.

FIFTEEN

Diaz finally left, and the house settled into quiet. Tony checked on the children every few minutes, even putting his palm on their backs to reassure himself that they were breathing easily.

Mara and Willow packed up clothing and food, and Austin readied the plane. He was still amazed at the steadfast help he'd gotten from the Duke family. Though their primary motive was keeping Willow safe, they'd stepped up at every turn for Tony and the kids also. If only Jude had the contacts and savvy to find a solution. Dread ebbed higher as he considered that there really was only one other answer, with Gaudy on the rampage. Find another place to hide, another name, another set of lies to teach the kids. A new life to take up...but this one would not have Willow Duke in it. For her own safety, he would likely never be able to contact her again. The thought cut a trail in his heart, spilling bitterness through his soul. He could run with the children, he'd done it before. But how could he run away from her?

Not the time, he told himself. He had to stay clear on the objective. Keep Willow and the kids safe until he got help from a trusted source. Twenty-four hours, tops, and Jude would arrive. He intended to savor every minute he could with her.

They waited until after the kids ate lunch before he led them to the plane. Austin gave them the thumbs-up. "Fully fueled and ready to go. Don't break it, huh? Cost me a mint."

"I won't," Tony said.

"I'll meet you there in a couple of hours."

Willow kissed her brother. "Did you get roped into protection duty again?"

He laughed. "I'm the night shift. Beckett's taking the day shift. Levi's on deck after that."

"A well-oiled Duke machine," she said.

"Yep." He helped Carter climb up and then lifted Bee while Tony took his seat behind the controls.

A glint from the tower caught Tony's eye. "Uncle Gino's keeping tabs on us."

Austin shrugged. "The cabin is plenty far afield. He won't find it."

Willow rolled her eyes. "Oh, of course.

We're going to Jude's man cave. I should have guessed."

"Have you been there before?" Tony asked.

"Only once. I helped with the construction. He bought the property after...well, things didn't go well with a woman in his life. It's built for solitude, which was Jude's intent. He doesn't invite people to visit very often. We know when he's in the mood to detach from the world."

Tony pulled on a pair of sunglasses. "Solitude sounds like exactly what we need right now."

Austin guided him out. As the plane picked up speed, he heard Carter gasp with delight. "Cool, Uncle Tony. We're gonna fly."

How rare it was to hear that serious child overflowing with excitement.

Carter's obvious delight warmed him. "Yes, it is cool," he said. "Want me to teach you to fly someday, Carter?"

"Yeah," Carter said. "Tomorrow."

Willow giggled. "Looks like you've got your first student. Maybe you should start a flight school."

"Maybe I should, someday." Though he knew it wouldn't last, he breathed in the sense of freedom, and possibility, the unfettered exaltation of soaring into a sizzling blue sky with a laughing boy, and a woman sitting next to him, her freckled face tipped to catch the sun. Never before had he felt the precious weight of his passengers. There was a big mess waiting for him on the ground, he knew, but up here there was peace. He allowed himself to enjoy the remainder of the flight, listening to Carter exclaim over everything he saw and Willow chatting easily. With regret, he finally dropped to a lower altitude in preparation to land.

The terrain was a series of low hills, rippling veins of mineral-deposited rocks with the mountains in the backdrop. The coordinates he'd been given led them to a small patch of trees snuggled near what must be some underground water source. A small wood-sided cabin rested in the shade of that oasis, served by a winding dirt road. There were no other structures anywhere around. Jude did indeed value his privacy.

He located the long stretch of paved ground Austin had insisted Jude put in so he could land a plane there. Jude, he'd been told, had grumbled over every detail and penny spent, but he called upon Austin from time to time to help fly in materials for improvements.

Tony glided the plane to a smooth stop, only a short distance from the cabin. There was really no way to hide the aircraft. If Gaudy's people were searching from the air and happened upon the location...

But they wouldn't. Death Valley was three thousand square miles of hostile terrain. Even with GPS devices people had gone missing in this wild place. And they'd told no one, not Diaz, nor Gino. Only Austin, Levi, Beckett and Jude knew where they were headed. The sun blazed down as he helped everyone out and hastened them inside. "I'll come back for the supplies."

Pushing open the door, he was surprised at the modern touches. The small living room was equipped with a tidy wood-burning stove. The kitchen boasted a propane-powered stove and refrigerator. There was a small bedroom in addition to a regular sofa and futon in the living room. Plenty sufficient for the brief time they would be there.

Leaving Willow inside with the children, he climbed to a peak of rock a hundred yards from the property. Through his binoculars, the view revealed sprawling desert acres and a deserted road. Two miles away he could barely make out the shingled roof of the lone neighbor. The only movement came from a hawk winging its way across the brilliant blue. Quiet. Isolated.

Satisfied he returned with the supplies.

"Look," Willow said, pointing to Carter. He'd found a die-cast plane figurine on the shelf and was zooming it around the room with accompanying sound effects.

"I don't think Jude will mind if he plays with it," she said.

Tony laughed and helped Willow unload the supplies. Bee was happy to see her bag of blocks. She stuffed Moo under her arm and sat down to play.

"So far so good," Willow said. "How about some dinner?"

"Great. I'll help if it's something that requires limited culinary skills."

She held up eggs and pancake mix. "Looks like breakfast for dinner."

"Perfect."

He did what he could to mix the batter and wash the utensils, enjoying his proximity to her as they produced the meal. As much as he tried, his mind would not stay on the happy domestic details and he burned a pancake before he realized it.

Willow expertly removed the charred cake with a spatula. "Worried about your brother?"

He sighed. "Worried about everything."

She turned off the burner, set the pancakes aside and took his hand. "Only one thing to do about that." Head bowed, eyes closed, she led them in a prayer. After the amen, she stood on tiptoe and cupped his cheek with her hand.

"Feel better?"

He gazed at her, wrapped in warmth he could not understand, and though nothing had changed, he felt something unusual, an unexpected sensation he could not identify at first.

Better didn't capture it. He felt...content.

He had no right whatsoever to feel that way, yet he did.

"Yes," he said, the lingering warmth from her touch buzzing his cheek. He wanted to stay there and keep the sensation alive, but she'd carried the pancakes to the table and set about distributing them. He said grace and began cutting food into child-sized pieces, while his thoughts still circled around Willow, Ron and the danger they'd only narrowly avoided.

She finally caught his attention with her laugh.

"What?"

"Thanks, Uncle Baloney, but I can handle cutting my own food."

He realized he'd reached out to cut her pancake into strips. Cheeks warm, he slid the plate back to her. "Sorry. Uncle habit."

They all joined in a good laugh as they dove into their meals.

As he cleaned the dishes afterward, Willow sat in the rocking chair with Bee, singing something about spiders and waterspouts. Carter flew his toy plane over the coffee table. Willow had switched on a lantern which supplemented the light from the small lamp. Everything was bathed in a soft glow. He closed his eyes and imagined this was real, normal and they were a family.

His eyes jerked awake a moment later when his phone buzzed. Nerves kicking to life, he checked the screen and sighed. "Your brother. He's five minutes out." He showed her the screen. "He thought he'd send a photo to reassure us it really is him."

Austin had somehow acquired a fake nose-eyeglass disguise, which made both Willow and Carter laugh. Good to experience the levity where they could. Besides, Tony knew Austin would be arriving armed, just in case.

He peered through the curtain until Austin's truck rolled up and opened the door for him.

After a hearty greeting for everyone, Austin ate a stack of pancakes and read a story to Carter while Willow put Bee down on the bed.

"I'll sack out on the couch," he said. Tony was relieved when Austin snapped a trigger guard onto his rifle and put it on top of the fridge.

He caught Tony's look. "I'd never risk a curious kiddo getting hurt," he said.

"Thank you."

"One less thing for you to worry about."

"Every little bit helps."

Austin slugged him on the shoulder. "Gonna be okay, man. By this time tomorrow Jude will have arranged something for you and the kids."

Tony nodded. *You and the kids.*

Why did that comforting phrase leave him with a trickle of deep despair?

Willow crawled into bed with Bee and sang to her about the cow who jumped over the moon while Tony and Austin settled into the other room. Carter shared the futon with Tony, and Austin sprawled on the sofa. The cabin creaked and settled as the searing daytime temperatures cooled. The room was stuffy, and she eased out of bed to open the window a crack.

A warm breeze trickled in along with something else. Engine noise. Heart pounding, she tried to figure out if her senses were playing tricks on her, but the window did not give her a clear view of the road. Fear sent her scurrying to the bedroom door. She yanked it open to find Tony's hand raised to enter.

"Someone's coming," he whispered.

Her mouth went dry. "Maybe Levi?" But he would have texted Austin.

"Austin went out the back door and he's circling around."

They heard a vehicle grind to a stop.

A moment later a fist slammed on the cabin door. "Tony, let me in," a voice roared.

Tony looked as shocked as Willow felt.

He ran to the curtains and looked out. She closed the door to the room where Bee slept and joined him, wondering what in the world she was supposed to do.

"Ron," Tony bellowed through the door. "You shouldn't have come here."

"I…" Ron yelped.

"He's alone and unarmed," came Austin's voice.

"You either shoot me or I stay here shouting until someone opens the door," Ron said.

Tony looked at Willow. "I don't see we have much choice."

He pulled it open. Ron stood, dirty and disheveled, while Austin trained the rifle on him from behind.

"How did you find this place?" Tony demanded.

"Learned a thing or two from Gaudy. Used a backdoor internet connection to search all the properties owned by the Duke family and stumbled on this remote oasis in the desert. I figured the Dukes might stash you nearby and I was right."

Tony groaned. "Gaudy probably has a tracker on your phone. They can follow you here."

"Uh-uh. I ditched my phone after the helicopter ambush." His nostrils flared. "I'm smarter than you give me credit for, Tony."

Austin lowered his weapon. "I'm not sure about that," he said. "If you found us, others could too."

"Then let's make this quick. I've come for my kids," he said again.

"Quiet down before you wake them up," Willow admonished as Tony shoved his fingers through his hair.

Carter stirred on the futon.

Ron peered around Tony. "Aww, man. He's gotten so big," Ron said. Then he glared at Tony. "You can't keep them. They're not yours, and I'm taking them."

"Where?" Tony said, exasperated. "And don't tell me Mexico because you'll never make it, and neither will they."

"Daddy?" Carter said, sitting up and rubbing his eyes.

Ron's face softened and he pushed by Tony and went to his son. "Hey, big fella."

Austin slid the rifle behind him so Carter

would not have a view of it. Tony exchanged a desperate look with Willow. She knew what he was thinking. Bee and Carter were not Tony's kids. He could not keep them from their foolhardy father.

They would have to convince him.

"Ron," she said softly. "Carter and Bee have been through a trauma. Klee tried to get us at our hiding place. They need time to rest and recover, and Bee has a cold. With her asthma, she shouldn't…"

He didn't appear to hear. "We're going to go on a trip," he said to Carter. "Won't that be fun? Me and you and sissy."

Austin was stepping inside when the door slammed open. Willow cried out as Uncle Gino charged in, a gun in his hand. He looked around and ordered Austin to put down his rifle. Grudgingly, Austin did so.

Perspiration slicked Gino's forehead. "Well, ain't this sweet? Finally got the two brothers together. A family reunion."

Willow stared in horror. Uncle Gino really was a traitor.

Tony grabbed Willow's arm and pulled her behind him. Ron stood between Gino and Carter. "I don't know what you think you're doing," Tony said calmly, "but there are two children in this cabin. Put away your gun, Uncle Gino."

"I'd love to, but it looks like it's up to me to take care of this situation so they can get out of it alive. You," he said to Austin. "Get over there with her. I'm here for Ron. Everybody stays calm and no one gets hurt."

Carter crawled out of the bed. "Daddy?" he said uncertainly, looking at Uncle Gino.

"Come here, Carter," Willow said. "Let's go into the bedroom with Bee."

But Carter stood still and staring.

"You've been betraying us all along," Willow said.

Gino shook his head. "Like I told you, it was the nurse. Diaz confirmed today that Gaudy's people got into the clinic database and cancelled the real nurse's appointment. They altered the credentials, faked an ID and dispatched Inez to the airstrip."

She remembered the glitch in the computer systems when the doctor was examining Bee. Gaudy had sent in a fake nurse to disable the alarm for Klee. And she'd bought the act completely.

"She led Klee right to you," Gino said, as if he read her thoughts. "Might as well have sent up a signal flare."

Signal. Something crept into her consciousness, but she could not bring it to the forefront.

"How did you track Ron?" Tony asked.

"He's not the only one with cyber smarts. Everybody needs gas, don't they? I figured sooner or later, Ron would refuel somewhere within a fifty-mile radius, so I put out feelers to all the local gas station owners to alert me if they saw anyone matching Ron's description fueling up. It was easy to catch onto his trail with a starting point. The marshals will figure it out too, eventually, but I beat them to the punch while Diaz was busy trying to clean up the mess from the helicopter ambush and Klee's tunnel attack."

"You lied, didn't you?" Tony said. "Told those station owners you were still a state trooper to get them to cooperate."

"I'm not going to apologize for doing what I had to do, Tony. You gotta break the eggs to make the omelet."

Though Willow tried to prevent him, Carter crept close to Ron and wrapped his arms around his father's leg. Ron patted his head. "Go into the bedroom with your sister, Carter."

"You said we were goin' on a trip," Carter said, raising his tearstained face. "I want to go now."

"I have to talk to Uncle Gino first," Ron said. "Just the grown-ups."

Carter refused to let go, burying his face in his father's pant leg. "Daddy," he said. And then he looked at Gino, his voice small and defiant. "Don't hurt my daddy."

Gino didn't lower the gun. "Do what your father says, son."

Tony slowly took Carter's hand and eased him away from Ron, enveloping him in a hug as he sobbed.

"What are you going to do with me?" Ron asked.

Gino shook his head. "So smart and so dumb at the same time. You never stopped a moment to think how your actions affected your brother, your kids. Look at your boy. Doesn't even understand the mess you've caused him."

Ron's mouth trembled. "I'm here to make it right."

Gino shook his head. "You're unbelievable, you know that? Your presence here is a beacon for Gaudy to follow. I found you—so will he. Well, I'm gonna shortcut that process."

A beacon. Again the nebulous thought, nibbling at Willow. What was her brain trying to tell her?

"What are you saying, Gino?" Tony asked.

"I've made a deal with Gaudy."

Willow felt her heart flip over as Gino continued.

"I hand over Ron, and he'll leave off you and the kids."

"No," Tony said. "You can't do that."

Gino snorted at Tony. "You're too soft, where your brother is concerned, you always have been. That's why I had to make the deal. Ron's life in exchange for yours and the kids. It's the only way. The longer I wait to meet them, the more likely it is that they'll track us and find you."

Signal. Beacon. Find you.

Her mind flashed back to the moments when Inez was alone with Bee.

The speed with which Klee had found the tunnel and pursued them. Dread solidified in her stomach and she fought to keep her lungs working. She was mistaken, paranoid, seeing conspiracies where there were none.

Oh please, don't let me be right.

She whirled and raced to the bedroom, praying she was wrong.

SIXTEEN

Tony figured Willow must have heard Bee cry out. Right now, he was frantically trying to come up with a plan. Gino wouldn't budge. Tony knew enough about his uncle to realize Gino wasn't going to leave without taking Ron with him unless he was physically unable to do so. Carter clung close as a limpet, his tears dampening Tony's T-shirt.

Austin eased a step closer until Gino growled at him.

"You can forget any ideas you have about getting the jump on me. I don't want to hurt you, since your family has been good to Tony and the kids, but I'm going to do what I have to do, understood?"

"This isn't the way," Austin said. "You don't sacrifice your own kin."

"Yes, you do, if that's the only way to save the rest. Tony, take the kid to the bedroom with his sister."

"I want to stay with Daddy," Carter said. His lip trembled.

"It's okay, son." Ron smiled at Carter and gave him a shaky thumbs-up. "We'll work this all out."

"We can come up with something," Austin was saying. "If you give us some time."

Gino's reply was interrupted by Willow's return. She wore an expression of utter defeat, Moo clutched in one hand.

Tony turned to her, heart hammering. "What's wrong?"

"I'm sorry. I didn't figure it out until just now." She held up the toy, pulled back the ribbon around its neck. A small metallic square glinted in the lantern light.

"A tracker?" Tony said, throat gone tight.

Willow nodded miserably. "The nurse put it on while I was getting her a glass of water. That's how Klee found the tunnel. He followed the tracker she planted. I'm so, so sorry."

Gino groaned aloud. "Then they'll be here anytime."

Without warning, a chopper's rotors vibrated the walls of the cabin. Before Tony could react, the windows exploded with gunfire. Uncle Gino cried out, blood pouring from his shoulder and the gun spiraling away as he fell. Austin dove to the floor, yanking Ron down with him. Tony pulled Willow low, grabbed Carter and pushed them toward the bedroom.

"What do I do?" Willow cried.

"Get Bee. Head for the back. Be ready to run."

"But…"

"Hurry, Willow." She ran for Bee, bundling her up and taking Carter's hand.

Tony looked out at Austin, who'd taken up a position to the side of the window with his rifle.

Through the cracked glass, Tony heard Klee shouting. "You said I could have the boy, Mr. Gaudy. Quit blasting up the place or you'll kill him."

Austin returned fire and the helicopter moved off a few yards, but Tony could just make out Klee through the broken glass. Klee raised an arm and lobbed something inside. The metal canister hit the floor with a clatter and the room began to fill with smoke.

"Now let me go in and get 'em," Klee shouted. "No need for shooting."

"Get them out, now," Austin shouted to Tony. "I'll buy as much time as I can."

Tony shielded Willow and the kids as best he could with his body, guiding, urging, cajoling them along through the smoke toward the back door. Staying low, they kept to the perimeter.

"Is Gino alive?" he called to Ron through the smoke.

"Yeah, but he's bleeding heavily." Ron dropped to his knees and tied his jacket around Gino's bleeding shoulder.

"Get him out the back. I'll bring Willow and the kids," Tony yelled.

Ron picked Gino up and tossed him over his shoulder. He stumbled to the back door.

A burst of gunfire raked the living room. Tony protected them as they crouched. They reached the back door and he urged Willow and the kids out into the cleaner air. He couldn't see where Ron or Uncle Gino had gone, but wherever they were, it was safer out than in. The hiding places were limited behind Jude's property, a small shed, and a stack of palettes, the woods beyond.

Several yards from the house, he pulled them behind the palettes. Willow crouched with a whimpering Bee. "Moo," she cried. "Want Moo."

"We'll get him soon," Tony soothed.

Carter's expression was pinched as if he might begin to sob at any moment. Not surprising after seeing his father held at gunpoint and the cabin shot to pieces all around him. Willow's blue-gray eyes were wide with shock. He gripped her shoulder.

"Head for the plane. Lock yourself inside and stay down. Jude's almost here so it won't be for long."

"What about you?" Tears dotted her cheeks. "You and Austin?"

"I'm going to help him, however I can." He quirked a smile. "You've already done your part, Willow."

"Tony," she half sobbed. Whatever she'd meant to say was lost in a gulp as she tried to pull her emotions under control. He knew she would dig down into that deep well of courage and compassion and do what was necessary to save the children, while her heart broke for Tony and her brother. Rock and a hard place. But Willow had been through hard places and her resolve was sturdier than any granite. Reaching out, his let his fingers trail over the smooth curve of her cheek, now damp with warm tears.

"I'm so sorry for all of this."

She shook her head. "Not your fault."

He tipped her chin up with a finger and kissed her, the softness of her lips warming him like a sunrise. "Like I said, you're the bravest person I've ever met. I am privileged that God allowed me to know you."

She stifled a sob and he kissed Bee on the cheek and knelt before Carter. "I'm going to go help your daddy and Austin. You take care of Willow and your sister, okay?"

Carter flung his arms around Tony, dropping his metal plane. Willow picked it up as Tony cradled Carter.

Tony bridled at the injustice of it. How unfair to ask so much of a scared boy, a baby girl and a woman who'd done nothing but suffer for them. But there was no other choice, no other way to save them.

"Go now," he said.

Not allowing himself to watch, he whirled around and raced back through the smoke. Reentering the cabin, he plowed through the haze, keeping as low as he could. Austin fired again out the shattered window.

"Jude caught an earlier flight, he's almost here and Diaz is en route too. We have to slow them down," Austin shouted. Muttering, he paused to reload his weapon as Klee hurtled through the window. He fell onto his knees and Tony didn't hesitate. He picked up a chair and brought it down on Klee's shoulders, breaking all four wooden legs with the effort.

Klee grunted and rolled away from the impact. Austin finished loading and aimed a shot at Klee, who fired first, sending Austin retreating into the hallway and Tony diving for cover behind the sofa.

Klee continued to shoot, carving holes into Jude's living room paneling. He stopped abruptly as gunfire from outside sprayed through the cabin. Tony felt the bullets penetrating the wood and foam.

"I can't believe I'm being double-crossed like this," Klee roared.

Get down, Tony wanted to shout, but Klee stood, like the figurehead on a ship defying the tumult around him.

"You said I could have the boy, Gaudy," he shouted out the window. "Jeffie is mine, remember? A deal's a deal." A shot struck him, and he cartwheeled backward, falling behind the futon and stayed there, unmoving.

"Come out and surrender," came a voice broadcast over the helicopter's speaker, "and we'll stop firing."

Austin threw himself down behind the sofa with Tony. "Jude's at the crossroads. Five minutes, tops."

"We'll be dead in five minutes unless we surrender."

Austin considered that. "Normally, I'd say no way, but I'm out of ammo and they're gonna come in shooting. Willow and the others need time to get as far away as they can."

"Agreed."

Austin sucked in a breath. "All right then.

Seeing as how I have a gorgeous wife to go home to, I guess surrender is the only option that means we possibly don't die. Needles me, though."

"I don't like it either," Tony said.

Austin's mouth tightened but he nodded. "We'll hope they mean what they say."

"I'll go," Tony said. "This is my family mess. Let me walk out alone."

Austin smiled. "Nah. You're an honorary Duke. We ride together, flyboy. Let's do this."

As they crawled out from the ruined sofa, Tony peered around the edge of the futon. Klee was lying there, still, curled into the fetal position. Wounded? Dead? Shot down by his own boss. No honor among thieves.

He didn't dare take a moment longer to render aid or consider the reality that Gaudy might just gun him and Austin down on sight. "We're coming out," he yelled. "Don't shoot."

Tony stepped past the threshold, hands in the air. He expected at any moment to feel bullets plowing into his chest. The lights from the helicopter blinded him, but he pressed on as slowly as he dared. After a few moments he heard Austin following.

"Stop," Gaudy commanded. Tony's vision gradually adjusted as the light beamed at him was lowered. Gaudy stood next to a woman with dark hair, twisted into a braid. Next to him was an armed man, gun pointed at Tony. Another watched from the helicopter cockpit. Of course Gaudy had brought plenty of people to watch his back. The Maestro didn't go anywhere unprotected.

Gaudy smiled. "Thanks for coming out. Saves us some ammo." The tough words seemed wrong coming from this slight, bespectacled man, as if he was playacting. The wreckage behind them said otherwise. There was nothing playful about what was going to happen.

"Who are you?" Tony said to the woman.

She shifted but didn't answer.

"This is my wife, Eugenia," Gaudy said. "I gave her the chance to make reparations for her infidelity by helping. She used to be a nurse, you know."

A nurse. "You left the tracker in Bee's toy?"

She nodded. "I—I had to cooperate," she said, so low he almost didn't catch the words.

No doubt. She had to do whatever Gaudy said if she was going to stay alive. She had good reasons, but all the same she'd almost cost him Willow and the children.

"Enough chitchat. Where's Ron?" Gaudy demanded. "Is he dead?"

Tony gritted his teeth. "You shot out the

windows and then Klee added the smoke. I'm not sure where Ron is."

"And your uncle Gino?" He flicked a hand toward Gino's car. "I didn't think he would be here too, but more's the better."

"Shot. Klee too, I think."

Gaudy shook his head. "Just as well. Klee was getting obsessive about the boy." He jerked a pointy chin at the cabin. "If I don't have Ron and his kids in my sights in two minutes, I will start shooting up the place until I am satisfied everyone is dead."

In the distance, Tony thought he caught the movement of a car with no lights racing up the dirt road. Jude, had to be, but Tony needed to buy more time. "I'll go in and get them," Tony said.

"Yes, you will," Gaudy said, taking a gun from his second in command. "And we're coming with you, just to be sure I'm the one that puts a bullet in him."

Gaudy flicked a finger at his pilot. "And to ensure there's no silliness, your friend here is going to stay."

The man from the cockpit emerged from the helicopter to train a gun on Austin. Gaudy probably did not trust Inez to do so.

Tony was going to protest, but Austin gave an almost imperceptible shake of his head.

Tony understood. Best to have the gun power split up, increasing the chances for Tony and Austin to help when the cops arrived.

"All right." Tony headed for the cabin.

Gaudy made sure to walk behind Tony and his number one. Typical cowardly move for someone who paid everyone else to break the law for him. Tony heard no further sounds of approaching law enforcement, but the wind had come up, tinkling the broken glass and flapping the ruined curtains. Tony pushed the door open slowly, mentally begging Jude to hurry. The smoke was still acrid, burning his nose, but it had begun to filter throughout the cabin and out into the night.

Gaudy's guard kept his gun trained, sweeping the room, but nothing moved.

"Where?" Gaudy said. "I don't see Ron or the kids."

"They're probably in the bedroom hiding," Tony said. "I'll go get them."

"No," Gaudy snapped. "You," he said to the guard.

The guard went into the hallway and bedroom, emerging a moment later. "No one in there, Mr. Gaudy."

"Check the back."

Tony's jaw clenched. Surely Willow and

the kids had moved clear, but he was not sure where Ron and Gino might have gone.

The guard hustled to the back door and strolled out, disappearing for a moment before he called, "Out here, Mr. Gaudy."

Tony went cold.

Gaudy urged him forward. They walked outdoors and moved toward the guard who was holding his gun at a spot behind the shed. With a sick feeling, Tony preceded Gaudy until he could see what the guard was staring at. Ron crouched next to Gino, who was limp, a pool of blood spreading from under his shoulder. Ron was pressing hard on the wound, trying to staunch the flow.

Gaudy laughed. "Finally, we're at the end of this thing, Ron. It has been a game of cat and mouse, but that just makes it more satisfying, right?"

Ron didn't move, staring insolently at Gaudy.

"What's the matter? At a loss for words?" Gaudy asked. "You won't ever live to blackmail me for one thin dime. You've got nothing."

Ron shook his head. "No, you have nothing. There isn't anyone who will stand next to you unless you pay them to."

"So high and mighty?" Gaudy's expression went livid. "Your kids won't even remember you, if I choose to let them live. If I wasn't pressed for time, I would kill them and make you watch."

Ron tensed, and Tony tried to figure out if he was close enough to sweep out a leg and knock Gaudy over. He wasn't, and the guard was also a cautious distance away.

"Stand up, why don't you?" Gaudy said. "Die like a man, even though you lived like a worm."

Ron got to his feet, Gino's blood staining his shirt and hands. "I'm not done yet."

Gaudy tipped back his head and laughed. "Yes, you are and you're too thickheaded to know it." Gaudy aimed at Gino. "Guess we should start getting rid of the witnesses. I've never actually shot a man myself, but there's a first time for everything. You can watch them die, Ron. What a treat for you, right?"

Without warning, Ron exploded like a charging rhino, straight at Gaudy. The motion took him by surprise. He toppled backward. Before the guard could step forward to help, Tony clocked the guard in the chin with a right cross that sent him to the ground in a limp heap.

Ron leaped on Gaudy, pinning his arms and wrenching the gun away. There was no contest between Ron's fury-driven strength and Gaudy's tremoring muscles. In the space of a moment, he'd stripped the gun and tossed it aside before he turned Gaudy on his belly and knelt on his legs, panting in his ear. "I told you I wasn't done. Now who's the smart one, right?"

Gaudy wriggled and grunted with rage, but Ron did not budge.

Tony stripped the unconscious guard of his weapon and tossed it with Gaudy's. He bent in half, steadying his breathing.

"The kids?" Ron said.

Tony regarded his brother. Ron was a man who'd made the worst decisions at the most critical junctures of his life, but it was clear that he loved his children with everything in him. "They're with Willow, at the plane."

Ron sighed. "I don't deserve you for a brother."

Tony quirked a smile. "Funny, I would say the same thing."

They both laughed. Tony could not remember the last time he'd laughed with Ron.

"That was impressive, you two." Uncle Gino reached a trembling hand out and wiped the sweat from his brows. He looked at Ron. "Why'd you carry me out here? You knew I was going to turn you over to Gaudy."

"What, that wasn't a bluff?" Ron said with a cocky grin that vanished quickly.

"You know it wasn't," Gino said, voice rough with pain. "So why'd you save me?"

Ron sighed. "Because I don't have one iota of common sense and you're family." Gino gasped in pain as Ron tried to tighten the jacket, which had slipped loose. "Now stay still, you stubborn goat, or you'll bleed to death."

Tony thought he saw the sliver of a smile on Gino's mouth as he closed his eyes.

Austin sprinted up, panting. "Cavalry's arrived. Jude and his people just arrested Inez and the guard. You okay? Where…?"

But Tony's attention was caught on something visible through the open door into the cabin. The futon had been pushed to the center of the room as the uniformed man Tony assumed was Jude entered the cabin and began to secure the premises with another officer.

He realized in a flash of terror that Klee was no longer lying behind the futon. He was alive, and he'd gone after Willow and the kids.

SEVENTEEN

Willow ran as fast as she could toward the plane, cutting through the trees, but their speed was a slow jog at best. Bee cried, and Willow had no breath to try and calm her. It was all she could do to keep Carter from falling and hold on to Bee while avoiding tree roots and patches of ground slick with pine needles.

She stopped in the shadows of a thick-trunked tree, cloaked from the moonlight. The shooting had stopped but she could no longer see the cabin from behind the swell of ground. At least she'd somehow managed to control the sobs that wanted to burst out of her. Austin, Tony... How would they survive with only Austin's rifle between them? When the panic began to swamp her, she forced it down.

The plane was only another twenty yards away. As soon as she caught her breath, it would be one more flat-out sprint and they'd climb in, lock up, hunker down until Jude arrived. When she got her gasping under control, she patted Carter's shoulder. "We're almost there."

"Where's Daddy? And Uncle Tony?"

She bit her lip and forced a smile. "They'll be here soon. They'd want us to keep going, right?"

Carter looked doubtful. "I think we should go back and get them."

"We will, I promise, but we have to wait in the plane."

Carter began to protest, but she was afraid to delay any longer. "We can do it." She took his hand and half lugged him away from the tree. The smooth white outline of the plane made her heart beat faster.

A couple of steps more.

Carter stumbled but righted himself and they covered the remaining ground to the paved strip and Austin's elegant aircraft.

She reached up to open the door when a voice froze her in place.

"There's my boy," Klee said. "Hey, Jeffie. It's Pops, come to get you."

She turned so quickly she almost dropped Bee. Klee stood in the moonlight, a dark shadow of blood staining his shirt. Throat almost closing in panic, she tried to pull Carter behind her.

"He's not your boy," she said.

"Yes, he is," Klee said. "Gaudy promised, and I'm gonna collect even though he served me up like a Christmas goose. He's gonna pay for that later." He smiled down at Carter. "Hello, Jeffie. Come to Pops, huh? We'll go find us a good place to go fishing."

Carter recoiled. "I'm not Jeffie."

"Awww, you will be. Just give it time."

Willow searched Klee's hands but did not see a gun. Would she be strong enough to fight him off? Normally probably not, but he was wounded and Willow felt a swell of fierce strength welling up inside of her along with a plan, a better way to stall for time. "How are you going to get out of here? The cops are on their way."

He shrugged. "I'll figure it out."

"You could fly," she suggested.

"Dunno how."

"I do." It was an exaggeration, but Austin had taught her the basics of taking off and landing. "I'll load the kids into the plane and I'll fly us out of here. Drop you wherever you want to go."

His eyes narrowed. "And why exactly would you do that?"

"Because I don't want Carter to get hurt and he's too tired to walk through the desert at

night. There are coyotes, snakes, scorpions—
not to mention it's going to get very cold tonight."

Klee considered that. "All right. You load
them up and fly us out of here. If you try anything, it will go badly for little sweet cheeks
there," he said, pointing to Bee. "And if you
think I'm not up to the task, take a gander
at this." He pulled a knife from his pocket.
"I may not have a gun, but I always have a
backup plan."

She swallowed, praying her own plan would
work. She just needed a minute shielded from
his view. With shaking hands she opened the
door and lifted Carter into the plane. "Sit
down, honey."

He stood there, frozen, until she gently
shoved him to the seat. "Please. It will all be
over soon," she whispered.

She picked up Bee and bundled her in next
to Carter. As she did so, she quickly detached
the fire extinguisher from the bracket. One
chance. One moment. All that stood between
Klee and the children.

"Oh Lord," she prayed under her breath.
"We need you now."

"Hurry up," Klee said. "I hear sirens."

"Almost got their buckles done," she called
over her shoulder. She eased the pin out of the

extinguisher and readied the nozzle. Giving herself a quick count of three, she whirled, spraying the liquid in a wide arc.

Klee had drawn closer, and the stream caught him by surprise, sending him stumbling back. She followed up by swinging the metal cylinder as close as she could to his head.

His stumble caused her to miss and the momentum sent her pitching onto her knees, the extinguisher rolling away.

Klee swiped his forearm over his eyes and in dismay she realized he still had possession of his knife. His face beamed hatred at her, hand clutching the hilt. "You lied too. Not going to forgive that. I'll take my boy and we'll walk out of this desert, but there's no need for you and the girl anymore."

"No," she screamed, ducking back from his slashing knife. But there was nowhere to run. She was jammed against the side of the plane as Klee bore down on her.

"Klee," a voice thundered.

Tony? Blinking, she saw him running through the trees. Klee turned slightly to look as Tony skidded within a few feet.

"Get away from my family," Tony said, through clenched teeth.

"The boy's..."

"Shut up," Tony snapped. "You're not taking him, and you're not hurting any of them."

Klee laughed. "Whatcha gonna do about it?"

Tony snatched a tree branch from the ground and swung it at Klee, who danced back.

"Nice, but a twig ain't gonna save you."

Willow crept toward the extinguisher, muscles rigid with fright. She grabbed it, but Tony and Klee were locked in a deadly standoff. Klee stabbed as Tony parried with the tree branch.

She crept from underneath the plane, clutching the extinguisher. Tony shot her a warning look, which she ignored. Klee raised the knife and bellowed, rushing with the blade aimed at Tony's throat.

Tony feinted to the side and used the branch to sweep the legs out from underneath Klee. He went down with a whoosh, and Willow saw her chance. She whacked Klee on the head. There was a dull thud. His eyes flickered and closed.

Heart thundering, she stood there while Tony checked him. "He's breathing. Unconscious."

She still expected him to leap up at any moment and come after them again.

Tony used Klee's belt to fasten his hands behind his back before he opened the door of the plane. Carter jumped into his arms. "Uncle Tony, you came back. Where's Daddy?"

"He's waiting for you," Tony said, voice husky as Willow freed Bee from her seat.

"Bloney," she squealed.

"Uncle Baloney is happy to see you too," Tony managed.

Willow hardly had the strength to move, but Tony guided them away a few yards and texted Austin.

"We'll stay here," he said, drawing her close. Carter sat on the ground with Bee in his lap. "Jude will be here momentarily."

She couldn't answer, and he didn't seem to be waiting for a reply. Then he was leaning in, kissing her and she felt as if her hammering heart would explode.

"Willow," he breathed, looking into her eyes. "I thought I'd lost you." He stopped and kissed her again until they were both breathless.

There was no way she could capture the wild sensations stampeding through her, the relief, the longing. Instead, she tried hard not to sob.

"Are you hurt, honey?" he whispered.

"I'm okay. The kids too."

He pulled her close, and ruffled Carter's and Bee's hair with his free hand before resting his chin on her head.

"Thank You, God," he whispered. And her heart added its own silent gratitude.

The night passed into early morning in a fog of details. Jude took charge of the crime scene, without much interference from Marshal Diaz, except that the marshals handled Gaudy's arrest and the transporting of Klee to the hospital. Tony insisted Willow and the children be checked by the paramedics Jude had summoned. A helicopter airlifted Uncle Gino to a Las Vegas hospital. Tony stood next to his brother, Willow and the kids on his other side until Jude finished his initial questions. The officer was clearly a Duke, strong, tall, with flashing blue eyes and a quick wit.

Jude shot a pained look at the still-smoky wreck of his cabin. "This is why I don't invite people over."

Tony had to laugh at that one. Still, though, he could not take his eyes off Willow for more than a few seconds. She was alive, unharmed, but his brain did not fully believe it.

The Dukes began to arrive quickly, Levi and Mara, Beckett and Seth. Mara took charge of the children, getting them settled in the Rocking Horse Ranch van.

"Pilar's prepping things at the airstrip so at least they can sleep tonight." Mara quirked a look at Jude. "That's safe, right? Will Gaudy be able to regroup and send more people from jail? Or should we move them elsewhere?"

Tony shook his head. The notion that had been lurking beneath more pressing thoughts would no longer be ignored. It was like watching a bad movie all over again. Gaudy would be arrested, and Ron would be a witness. Tony might be called on to testify as well. He shot a look at Bee and Carter. Who would care for the kids? He could refuse to testify, as his brother had done. Would Gaudy again dispatch people to enact revenge on Ron, Tony, possibly the Dukes? Had the situation become worse instead of better?

Diaz broke in. "It's fine for tonight. Jude's got officers to secure the place and Gaudy's going to be in jail for at least twenty-four hours as we get the ball rolling. Now we've got him on attempted murder so the DA has a whole new case to prepare, which will take months. For a few nights, the airstrip is fine until we can assess new threat levels."

Threat levels.

Diaz stared at Ron. "You would still be a key witness since you know the most about his business dealings. Are you going to testify this time without bugging out on us? You have to understand now that there is no other way to neutralize Gaudy but to send him to prison."

Ron blew out a breath and Tony tensed, awaiting his answer.

"Yes, I'll give you the info I have on him and I'll testify," he said finally. Turning to Tony he sighed. "I should have done what was right in the first place. I guess you got all the good genes in the family. Uncle Gino always said you were the smart one."

Tony clasped his brother's shoulder. "You stood up for your kids and Uncle Gino when the bullets started flying."

"Daddy," Carter called from the van.

A smile lit Ron's face. "I'll go say goodbye to the kids before I head to the hospital. I don't want Uncle Gino to terrorize the nurses too much."

"We'll send you with a marshal escort, and alert hospital security," Jude said. "As a precaution."

The truth was that Uncle Gino was probably headed into emergency surgery after massive blood loss. Tony knew he might not survive. "I'll go too." Tony turned to Levi and Austin. "Will you two stay with Willow and the kids tonight?"

Austin nodded. "Sure thing, Tony."

Tony took Willow's hand, trying to think

how to put everything he felt into words. She beat him to the punch. "It's not over, is it?" Her face was so pale in the strobing police lights.

"No," he forced himself to say. "But no matter how this goes from here, you've done everything you could."

"I can…"

He stopped her. "You almost died, Willow. You sacrificed yourself to save the kids and that's a debt I can never repay."

What was he doing, ending things right now? But he knew as he looked into those tear-glistened eyes that he could not, must not, ask her to stay by his side. She would never be safe, and he could not give her the future she richly deserved.

Willow swallowed and he leaned in to kiss her. His heart longed to spill out how he truly felt about the incomparable woman in front of him. But Diaz's phrase tied his tongue.

Threat levels.

He slid his hands over her shoulders and allowed himself one more kiss. "Thank you, Willow," he whispered.

He turned quickly, before she could see the moisture forming in his eyes. Anger, resentment, the injustice of it, all faded away into a smoky cloud of despair.

He loved her too much to ask her to stay with him.

Heart ripped into pieces, he forced himself to walk away.

The next morning she awoke to find it already hot. Sun streamed over the rollaway, and she reached for Bee. Her searching fingers found only an empty bed. She sat up. Heart pounding, she ran into the next room. Two more empty cots. Whirling, she plowed into Mara, who was entering the room.

"Where are they?"

She clasped Willow's arm. "Whew, you're up finally."

"Mara," Willow snapped. "Where are Tony and the kids?"

Mara's dark eyes were gentle. "Honey, they left."

"Left where?"

"We weren't told…for security reasons. Diaz arranged another location and identity for them until the new trial concludes."

Willow felt her lungs deflating. She could still feel their shared kiss, and the memory of how her heart responded to Tony in that moment. "But I didn't get to say goodbye."

Mara wrapped her in an embrace. "I know. I'm so sorry."

"So that's it?" She sank onto the empty bed. "I'll never see them or know how they're doing?" She snapped her fingers. "Just like that, they're out of my life?"

Mara sat next to her. "Completely wrong and unfair, but there's no way to guarantee Gaudy won't start up another campaign of terror."

"So what am I supposed to do?"

Mara said something encouraging, but Willow knew the real answer. *Pick up the pieces of your life and try to forget Tony and the children.* But how could she do that when her whole being cried out for them?

"What about Uncle Gino?"

"He's stable, survived the surgery. Doctors expect him to make a full recovery."

Escaping Mara's sympathetic gaze, she packed up her things, shoving them blindly into a duffel bag. When she saw the toy train left lying on the table downstairs, it was too much. Her eyes filled and she fled the apartment.

For two days she managed to avoid the well-meaning calls of her family, answering texts only when she had to. Drowning her sorrows in mint chip ice cream did not help. Nor did pulling weeds in her tiny apartment patio garden or taking long drives in the desert.

Work. That would fill up the hours. Though

she felt not the least flicker of excitement, she drove to her office, intending to bury herself in her computer files. It was the only thing she could think of to dispel the ache of Tony's absence. Where was he now? Was he struggling to find a new job? Childcare for the kids? Had he decided to put them in foster care like Uncle Gino had suggested? She flicked on the fan and slumped in her office chair, hands on her chin.

A knuckle rapped on the door.

A customer? She forced a businesslike smile and opened it, gasping in surprise.

"I heard a wonderful photographer works here, and we need a family picture," Tony said, holding Bee, Carter smiling next to him.

She gaped. Then she cried, hugging Carter and Tony and Bee together.

"I didn't think I would see you again." She flinched, quickly drawing them inside and closing the door. "Should I close the blinds? Is it safe for you to be here?"

Tony held up a finger. "I'll tell you everything in one second." He led Bee to a kid-sized chair and settled her. "All right, sweetie," he said, handing her a book from the basket of children's stories Willow kept there. "Uncle Baloney needs to talk to the pretty lady for a moment."

He fished the die-cast plane out of his pocket and gave it to Carter, who joined his sister.

"I'm getting better about traveling with toys," he said proudly. "Jude was nice enough to let Carter keep the plane. Actually, he was pretty cool about the destruction to his property also."

She blinked to be sure she wasn't imagining things. "How…? I mean…what…?"

Tony nodded. "My feelings exactly when Diaz came to visit me. I couldn't get a sentence out either, especially after her bombshell. Seems like her dreams of convicting Gaudy will never be realized."

"Why?"

"He's dead."

Her mouth fell open. "What? How did that happen?"

"Klee was being transferred to a holding facility when Gaudy was coming out of the booking area. He saw Gaudy and became enraged, attacking him before the officers could restrain him. He plowed head on into Gaudy and knocked him into the wall. Gaudy died of a brain hemorrhage."

She tried to assimilate that information. "That's awful."

"Yes. A terrible ending to the whole sorry

business. At least Klee will go to prison for what he's done."

She tried to struggle through the ramifications, but Tony interrupted her.

"I would not have wished Gaudy's death, but I have my life back now," he said, quietly. "Diaz and the DA will be pursuing other criminals on the dark web, though, with the assistance of another key witness."

"Who?"

"Klee. He was so angry that Gaudy betrayed him that he started to talk to the marshals. Turns out he's a pretty meticulous record keeper and he shared dates, times, transactions from all the dirty work he's done that will expose plenty of Gaudy's henchmen. There are other participants for the marshals to pursue also. I'm assured Klee is still going to prison, though, regardless of his cooperation."

She took a moment to absorb it. "Gaudy is gone, and Klee is going to prison." She fingerwiggle waved at the smiling Bee, who was holding the book up to the fan to watch the pages flutter. "So…what happens to the children? Is Ron taking them back?"

"Yes, eventually, but he's promised to live wherever I wind up settling, so the kids and I can stay close." He sighed. "And I can keep tabs on him. Uncle Gino found him a job book-keeping at a garage temporarily, and Ron's vowed to make it work. This time, I think he really means it."

She nodded. He was moving on. Part of her was glad and the other part ached that she would not be standing by his side. As much as she tried to tell herself that she was better off without Tony, her heart knew better. *Get used to it, heart.*

She offered a wan smile. "Where have you decided to move?"

"That depends."

"On what?"

Tony reached up and touched one of her curls that had come loose from the elastic. He looked at her dreamily, as if he'd lost his train of thought. "I forgot how much I love your hair when it refuses to stay where you want it to."

She fingered a strand nervously, confused. The scent of him, the nearness of him was almost too much to bear. She tried to edge back, but he encircled her wrists with his fingers. "I didn't figure on having anyone stop in the office today. I'm not really dressed properly."

He laughed. "I've seen you covered in grit, muddy, clawing to save two children you weren't even related to." He swallowed. "To save me." He reached up to run his fingers through the silky strands. "This is how I'll always think of you, hair loose and tumbling around all those freckles."

She stilled, no longer trying to wrangle the hair he'd set free. Her own heartbeat was a wild stampede now, as she looked at the man whom she'd gotten to know deeply, truly, in the midst of terrible danger.

"I love you," he said abruptly.

She pulled away, pressing her hands to her mouth, wondering if she was dreaming. He loved her? Maybe it was just gratitude, born of the trauma they'd been through. But he took her hands again, pressing a kiss tenderly to her knuckles and in his searching eyes she saw sincerity, deep commitment and the truest love she could imagine.

"Are you...sure?"

He laughed. "Am I sure? Let me put it to you this way—I am certain of only two things in this world, one is that the Lord loves me, and I love you." His smile faded. "But... I understand if you don't feel that way. I lied to you to pull you into my world. You have every right to kick me to the curb."

The weight of emotion made her close her eyes for a moment. It was not a dream. This man, her man, loved her in the same way she loved him, deeply, faithfully, in a way that would last for a lifetime. She cocked her head, a swirl of deep joy rising up and pouring through her. "Now why would I do that to the man I love?" she choked out.

His face lit like a Mojave desert sunrise. "No joke? I'm not dreaming, right? You really said that you love me?"

"No, joke, no dream. I love you too," she whispered. "Tony, or Anthony or Uncle Baloney, whatever your name is, I love you madly."

With hands that shook a bit, he pulled a ring box from his pocket. "I brought something for you too," he said, removing a gold band and dropping to a knee.

He threaded one hand with hers and held up their joined palms. "I know we started out with lies, but no more. Here is the absolute truth. You are the courageous, beautiful, woman of faith I have always wanted and in no way deserve. Will you marry me, Willow Duke?"

Tears and laughter rolled together. Overcome, she tried to rally an answer.

"Are you gonna say yes?" Carter chimed in. She giggled.

"Yes, Carter, I believe I will marry your uncle Tony." She allowed him to slip the ring on her finger.

Sighing, he jumped up and swept her into an enormous embrace, kissing her. He twirled her around and Bee squealed and clapped.

"What do you think, kids? Should we have a wedding with cake so Willow can be your auntie?"

"Cake," Bee sang out.

Carter nodded. "Will Daddy come?"

"Absolutely," Tony said. "And a whole bunch of Dukes too, I hope."

Willow grinned. "You get one Duke, you get them all."

"As long as I get you, that's fine by me."

Then he whirled and kissed her again.

"Know what?" Tony said, a smile wreathing his face. "I feel like having some ice cream to celebrate. Who's with me?"

Both kids shouted their agreement and they let themselves outside into the sizzling desert afternoon.

* * * * *

If you enjoyed this story,
look for these other Desert Justice books
by Dana Mentink:

Framed in Death Valley
Missing in the Desert
Death Valley Double Cross

Dear Reader,

Wow, what a ride! We have had four adventures so far in this Desert Justice series and there are two more to come. I really enjoyed writing this story about a man who has his choices taken away from him, forcing him to let go of the life he'd planned for himself. Yet Tony comes to know that the life God chose for him is so much richer and better than anything he might have picked for himself. My life has certainly been like that. Challenges that I never would have chosen have helped me grow and change. How about you? Have you experienced those "U-turns" that delivered you to a place where you could better know God? I hope so! And I hope you'll come along on the next adventure in the series!

As always, thank you very much for choosing to read my book. If you'd like to connect further, you can find me on Facebook, Book-Bub and on my website at danamentink.com. There is a physical address there as well if you prefer to reach out through the mail. Thank you again, and God bless!

Dana Mentink

Get 4 FREE REWARDS!

We'll send you 2 FREE Books plus 2 FREE Mystery Gifts.

FREE Value Over $20

Both the **Love Inspired**® and **Love Inspired**® **Suspense** series feature compelling novels filled with inspirational romance, faith, forgiveness, and hope.

YES! Please send me 2 FREE novels from the Love Inspired or Love Inspired Suspense series and my 2 FREE gifts (gifts are worth about $10 retail). After receiving them, if I don't wish to receive any more books, I can return the shipping statement marked "cancel." If I don't cancel, I will receive 6 brand-new Love Inspired Larger-Print books or Love Inspired Suspense Larger-Print books every month and be billed just $5.99 each in the U.S. or $6.24 each in Canada. That is a savings of at least 17% off the cover price. It's quite a bargain! Shipping and handling is just 50¢ per book in the U.S. and $1.25 per book in Canada.* I understand that accepting the 2 free books and gifts places me under no obligation to buy anything. I can always return a shipment and cancel at any time. The free books and gifts are mine to keep no matter what I decide.

Choose one: ☐ **Love Inspired Larger-Print**
(122/322 IDN GNWC)

☐ **Love Inspired Suspense Larger-Print**
(107/307 IDN GNWN)

Name (please print)

Address   Apt. #

City   State/Province   Zip/Postal Code

Email: Please check this box ☐ if you would like to receive newsletters and promotional emails from Harlequin Enterprises ULC and its affiliates. You can unsubscribe anytime.

Mail to the Harlequin Reader Service:
IN U.S.A.: P.O. Box 1341, Buffalo, NY 14240-8531
IN CANADA: P.O. Box 603, Fort Erie, Ontario L2A 5X3

Want to try 2 free books from another series? Call 1-800-873-8635 or visit www.ReaderService.com.

*Terms and prices subject to change without notice. Prices do not include sales taxes, which will be charged (if applicable) based on your state or country of residence. Canadian residents will be charged applicable taxes. Offer not valid in Quebec. This offer is limited to one order per household. Books received may not be as shown. Not valid for current subscribers to the Love Inspired or Love Inspired Suspense series. All orders subject to approval. Credit or debit balances in a customer's account(s) may be offset by any other outstanding balance owed by or to the customer. Please allow 4 to 6 weeks for delivery. Offer available while quantities last.

Your Privacy—Your information is being collected by Harlequin Enterprises ULC, operating as Harlequin Reader Service. For a complete summary of the information we collect, how we use this information and to whom it is disclosed, please visit our privacy notice located at corporate.harlequin.com/privacy-notice. From time to time we may also exchange your personal information with reputable third parties. If you wish to opt out of this sharing of your personal information, please visit readerservice.com/consumerschoice or call 1-800-873-8635. **Notice to California Residents**—Under California law, you have specific rights to control and access your data. For more information on these rights and how to exercise them, visit corporate.harlequin.com/california-privacy.

LIRLIS22

Get 4 FREE REWARDS!

We'll send you 2 FREE Books plus 2 FREE Mystery Gifts.

FREE Value Over **$20**

Both the **Harlequin® Special Edition** and **Harlequin® Heartwarming™** series feature compelling novels filled with stories of love and strength where the bonds of friendship, family and community unite.

YES! Please send me 2 FREE novels from the Harlequin Special Edition or Harlequin Heartwarming series and my 2 FREE gifts (gifts are worth about $10 retail). After receiving them, if I don't wish to receive any more books, I can return the shipping statement marked "cancel." If I don't cancel, I will receive 6 brand-new Harlequin Special Edition books every month and be billed just $4.99 each in the U.S or $5.74 each in Canada, a savings of at least 17% off the cover price or 4 brand-new Harlequin Heartwarming Larger-Print books every month and be billed just $5.74 each in the U.S. or $6.24 each in Canada, a savings of at least 21% off the cover price. It's quite a bargain! Shipping and handling is just 50¢ per book in the U.S. and $1.25 per book in Canada.* I understand that accepting the 2 free books and gifts places me under no obligation to buy anything. I can always return a shipment and cancel at any time. The free books and gifts are mine to keep no matter what I decide.

Choose one: ☐ **Harlequin Special Edition**
(235/335 HDN GNMP)

☐ **Harlequin Heartwarming**
Larger-Print
(161/361 HDN GNPZ)

Name (please print)

Address   Apt. #

City   State/Province   Zip/Postal Code

Email: Please check this box ☐ if you would like to receive newsletters and promotional emails from Harlequin Enterprises ULC and its affiliates. You can unsubscribe anytime.

Mail to the Harlequin Reader Service:
IN U.S.A.: P.O. Box 1341, Buffalo, NY 14240-8531
IN CANADA: P.O. Box 603, Fort Erie, Ontario L2A 5X3

Want to try 2 free books from another series! Call 1-800-873-8635 or visit www.ReaderService.com.

---

*Terms and prices subject to change without notice. Prices do not include sales taxes, which will be charged (if applicable) based on your state or country of residence. Canadian residents will be charged applicable taxes. Offer not valid in Quebec. This offer is limited to one order per household. Books received may not be as shown. Not valid for current subscribers to the Harlequin Special Edition or Harlequin Heartwarming series. All orders subject to approval. Credit or debit balances in a customer's account(s) may be offset by any other outstanding balance owed by or to the customer. Please allow 4 to 6 weeks for delivery. Offer available while quantities last.

Your Privacy—Your information is being collected by Harlequin Enterprises ULC, operating as Harlequin Reader Service. For a complete summary of the information we collect, how we use this information and to whom it is disclosed, please visit our privacy notice located at corporate.harlequin.com/privacy-notice. From time to time we may also exchange your personal information with reputable third parties. If you wish to opt out of this sharing of your personal information, please visit readerservice.com/consumerschoice or call 1-800-873-8635. **Notice to California Residents**—Under California law, you have specific rights to control and access your data. For more information on these rights and how to exercise them, visit corporate.harlequin.com/california-privacy.

HSEHW22

COUNTRY LEGACY COLLECTION

19 FREE BOOKS IN ALL!

Cowboys, adventure and romance await you in this new collection! Enjoy superb reading all year long with books by bestselling authors like Diana Palmer, Sasha Summers and Marie Ferrarella!

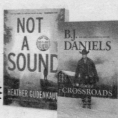